FROM AFAR

FOR ████ & ████
WITH LOVE

Roger Thomas

FROM AFAR

by

Roger Thomas

TUMBLAR HOUSE
' Bona Tempora Voluant'

Arcadia
MMXVI

Printed in the United States of America

ISBN 978-1-944339-06-7

From Afar

Visit our website at www.tumblarhouse.com

To my beloved Ellen, fellow laborer for 35 years.

With special thanks to David Thomas, PhD., Tom Doran, and Michael Richard for historical and editorial assistance and suggestions

Map of Alwenah Valley

AUTHOR'S NOTE:

The Parthian Empire in the early 1ˢᵗ Century A.D.

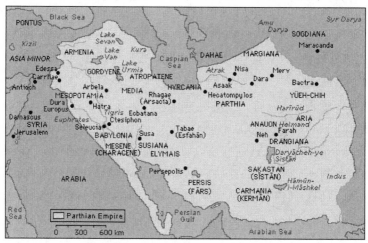

Map source: http://www.iranchamber.com/history/parthians/parthians.php

Among the most mysterious figures in all history are the Magi, or Wise Men, spoken of in the 2ⁿᵈ chapter of St. Matthew's Gospel. We don't know who they were, where they came from, what their names were, or even how many there were. They have been the source of endless speculation through the years, firing the imaginations and devotion of generations of students. But of all the questions raised by these mysterious figures, two stand out: what did they see in the heavens that impelled them to seek the King of the Jews, and why would pagan astrologers care about that King?

To address the first question, I've drawn heavily from the research of Rick Larson, an amateur astronomer whose site bethlehemstar.net recounts his use of star mapping software to go searching for what the ancients might have seen in the sky that would spark their interest. Since his hypotheses are compelling, and his research easily reproducible by anyone with the proper tools, I've taken it as the basis for the astronomical component of this tale.

The second question is more challenging. Looking back over millennia of salvation history, Christians can see the importance of the newborn King of the Jews. But such a perspective was anything but obvious to the people of the early 1st century. The Jews at that time were scattered and weak, lacking vast lands, strong leaders, a mighty military, or material wealth—in short, anything that made a nation impressive. Why any Gentiles would care about a newborn king of this weakened people is one of the biggest mysteries of the account.

I wish to thank David A. Thomas, PhD, of Northwest University for his expertise on the Hellenistic world, particularly the Parthian Empire. Any errors or misstatements are mine.

"Many nations will come from afar to the name of the Lord God, bearing gifts in their hands, gifts for the King of heaven. Generations of generations will give you joyful praise."

Tobit 13:11

VISITORS

"Once there was a potter who lived by a river. On the first day of each week he would go out and dig clay from the river bank. The next day he would wash the clay. The day after that he would form his pots, and then the next day he would fire them in his kiln. The following day he would paint the pieces, and the next day he would load them on his donkey to take them to market. The next day he would rest with his family before beginning again the following morning.

"The potter did this for years, training his son in the potter's craft. He kept the same schedule, dug the same clay, and even followed the same road from his house into town. But by the road stood a large tree. One day as the potter was passing beneath the tree, a great branch cracked and fell, scattering and breaking the pottery and killing the potter.

"His wife and son buried the potter and sang the dirges and offered the sacred meal and mourned him for the prescribed period. Then his son went out and dug the clay, washed it, formed it, fired it, painted it, and loaded the pots on his donkey to take to market, following the same road his father had."

The captain fell silent, and the guard looked at him as if expecting more. But the captain had finished. Eventually the guard asked, "That's—that's it?"

"Yes, Araxis, that's it," the captain answered. "It's called the Parable of the Potter. When I asked the master for a wise story, that's what he told me."

1

"But…" Araxis stammered. "What does it *mean*?"

The captain smiled. "That's what I asked him."

"What did he say?"

"He just smiled at me and said, 'When you figure it out, let me know.'"

Araxis pulled a face and sputtered. "But…but…how is that supposed to be wisdom? It doesn't even make any sense! I mean, I can understand it, but where's the mystical meaning?"

The captain stood up and clapped the guard on the shoulder. "When you figure it out, let me know."

"Captain Tigranes! Captain Tigranes!" A voice called, and the captain turned to see one of the slave boys come running.

"What is it, lad?"

"Lookout tower reports mounted party coming up the river road, sir," the boy gasped. "At least four, all armed and riding hard!"

"Four armed horsemen?" The captain asked, ruffling the boy's hair.

"And riding hard, sir!" The lad confirmed breathlessly.

"Well, then, let's take a look, shall we?" The captain said, heading for the watchtower. "Araxis, go join the guard at the gate, but don't panic."

Captain Tigranes headed along the inside of the estate wall toward the watchtower, the slave lad panting along behind. Again Tigranes blessed in his heart the architect of this estate house, who had combined elegance and beauty with serviceable practicality. The walls reached out from the cliff against which the manor nestled, sweeping in a smooth arc out to where the main gate opened onto the road, and then back to the tan cliffs again. The walls looked light and graceful, and only a trained eye could spot that they were wide enough for defenders to man the tops, and planted solidly in the rock to deny miners and sappers any advantage. The estate's towers soared gracefully above the gardens, catching cooling breezes from the mountains and river—and enabling the watchmen atop them to see far down the valley. The well-tended gardens grew as many edible plants as flowers, and the stables could hold many more cattle and goats in a pinch. The main gate was thick wood banded with iron, and had watchtowers above it. The estate might not be able to withstand a real siege by an actual army, but it would hold out against a band of brigands, which was the most likely threat here in the hills.

Tigranes mounted the watchtower, the slave lad following, not wanting to miss a moment of the excitement. Reaching the lookout platform, they found a guard peering attentively down the valley. The view was beautiful, with the Eulaeus river dancing down the slope to the valley floor with the river road running along its bank. Tigranes shaded his eyes to get a better look.

"So, what have we got here, Hymeas?" Tigranes asked the guard.

"Four horsemen, one clearly leading. Looks like a lord and his retainers. You can just see them coming clear of the bend now," Hymeas replied.

"Coming clear of the bend? You spotted them beyond the bend? Good work, man."

"Well, that was Baba here," Hymeas gestured to the slave boy. "He called my attention to them when they were just clearing the valley floor."

"Did you, now?" Tigranes clapped Baba on the shoulder. "Well done, lad."

Baba glowed at the praise. "And they're armed, sir! See their lances?"

"I do, just barely," Tigranes replied. "But notice that the lances are strapped to their saddles, not in their hands. Not what you'd expect from a hostile party. But let's go see. Baba, would you like to come?"

"Me? Yes, sir!" came the excited reply.

They made their way down to the main gate, Baba working to check his scurrying feet so he didn't run faster than the captain's unhurried strides. At the gate they found Araxis and the gate guard watching the horsemen, who could now be seen from ground level.

"Spears and shields, Captain?" the gate guard asked.

"Yes, but no armor," Tigranes replied. "And leave the gate standing open. I don't think our visitors are hostile—in fact, I'm beginning to have my suspicions about the leader."

The two guards ducked into the nearby arms locker, emerging with spears and shields and taking station on either side of the gate. Tigranes waved Baba back to a spot just inside the gates from which he could observe safely, but stayed directly in front himself, his hand on the hilt of his sword, watching the approaching party. The horsemen were coming on at a canter, and as they grew closer a smile slowly spread across Tigranes' face. When the riders were a furlong off and slowing to a walk, Tigranes beckoned Baba forward.

"Yes, sir?" Baba asked, nervously eying the oncoming riders.

"Take a message to the master, Baba."

"The master?" Baba asked in awe. Typically slaves didn't bring messages to the master himself.

"Yes. You were the first to spot them, so you can bear the good news. Tell the master that an old friend has arrived, one whom he may wish to come welcome."

"Old friend...come welcome..." Baba muttered as he dashed off. The riders were now within hailing distance, and the leader was holding up his right hand, palm outward.

"Guards, attention!" Tigranes called, drawing his sword and saluting sharply. They held that position until the riders pulled up before the gate. The leader, a trim but muscular man in dusty travel leathers, dismounted with practiced ease. He was a little shorter than most, but carried himself with easy grace. His hair and beard were closely trimmed, as if to fit easily within a battle helmet, and his skin was dark even by Parthian standards.

"Well, well, full martial honors," the man said, approaching with a broad grin.

"No less than your due, Lord Gudpharasa," Tigranes replied, grinning in return as he snapped down his salute.

"I hope I'm also due a handclasp," the lord replied, gripping the captain's forearm. "It is good to see you again, old friend."

"It has been too many years since you've graced these gates, my lord. I've sent word to the master, and I expect he will come to greet you personally. But can I make your retinue welcome?"

"Thank you. Gentlemen, may I present Captain Tigranes, chief of my Lord Melchior's guard. Captain, this is Gordias, Keos, and Tetius Caesius, my companions in arms."

The three men bowed deeply, and Tigranes saluted in return. "Any friends of Lord Gudpharasa are welcome in this house."

"Oh, Tigranes, for their sake use the shortened form. I go by Gaspar mostly these days, their poor Greek and Latin tongues struggling as they do with all those syllables."

"Very well, my lord. You're warmly welcome no matter what name you come under. But let us get out of the sun. Men, tend to our guests' horses."

The guards took the reins as the men removed their riding gloves and caps, slapping the road dust from their sleeves. As they passed through the gate, the three retainers looked in wonder at the well-tended groves and neat paths lacing the estate grounds.

"As always, a place of peace and gentle silence," Gaspar said. "We wanted so much to come up last night, but we made it into Seleucia late, and our poor horses needed the rest. We started as soon as we could this morning."

"Gudpharasa!" came a cry, and they looked up to see an older man scurrying down the path toward them, Baba close at his heels. Gaspar ran ahead and embraced the man warmly.

"And to think he was wondering if he'd be remembered," said Gordias with a smile.

"Lord Guda—Gaspar? Oh, certainly," Tigranes answered. "Master Melchior has had many students over the years, and remembers them all. But a handful were very close, almost like sons. Lord Gaspar was one of those." Up ahead, Gaspar and Melchior were walking toward the main house, heads together, engrossed in conversation and oblivious to all else.

"My apologies," Tigranes continued. "Usually my master welcomes all his guests in person, but as you can see, the delightful surprise of your master's arrival has preoccupied him. Permit me to welcome you in his name, and offer you all comfort. If you wish, you may supervise the stabling of your mounts, but be assured our grooms are skilled and treat all beasts as their own."

"Thank you, Captain," Keos said. "If your stables are run in half the good order that the rest of the estate seems to be, our horses are in the finest hands."

"Then let us see to your stabling," Tigranes replied. "Baba, run ahead and tell the chamberlain to prepare four rooms for our guests—and run baths as well."

"Rooms?" gasped Gordias. "Captain, we can barrack with your men, I'm sure—we're just common soldiers."

"If you are companions of Lord Gaspar, you are guests of the household, and that means rooms. Yours will be small ones, about the size of mine. Your lord will get the guest suite."

"The hospitality of Persia is legendary," said Gordias with another bow.

The sun was westering as the two old friends relaxed on the airy balcony overlooking the estate's garden.

"Your garden is magnificent as always, Melchior," Gaspar said. "I never appreciated how clever the channeling was, to divert water from the river down here into the estate."

"I have to give the prior owner credit for that," Melchior admitted. "His efforts made the estate self-sufficient for water. The channels not only feed the pools and fountains, but the kitchens and stables as well. We use the outflow to wash waste away into a ravine. Very well thought out."

"Yes, a few campaigns with the Romans teaches one the value of even such messy matters. They're scrupulous about their latrine arrangements," Gaspar confirmed.

"Ah, so you have ridden with the Romans. I suspected as much. You've been reticent to speak of what you've been up to, and I haven't wanted to press the point," Melchior said.

"I've been enjoying your hospitality and resting from our road-weariness," Gaspar explained. "It takes old campaigners like us a while to adjust to even being in a home, where ordinary people live out their ordinary lives."

Melchior laughed. "Only a blind man would call you an old campaigner. You're just twenty-five, aren't you? You have to be, because you've only been gone seven years, and you were eighteen when you left."

Gaspar sighed, and the shadows across his face in the fading daylight made him look twice his years. "Some ages cannot be measured by months. Yes, I've ridden far. I've seen the plains of Hispania and the forests of Gaul. I've ridden across Africa from Alexandria to the Gates of Hercules, and seen the shores of Britannia. I've seen Damascus and Ephesus and Athens and, of course, Rome. I've strategized with generals and advised proconsuls and served kings. I've seen deeds of nobility and heroism, and I've seen acts of unspeakable savagery done in the name of power and glory. Indeed, it seems like much longer than seven years."

"So you followed through on your plans, then?" Melchior asked.

"To the degree I could," Gaspar admitted with a shrug. "Your education was a fine base. You taught me how to think and observe and articulate. Your library on the campaigns of Alexander is one of the finest east of Alexandria itself. When I left here I sought out the best libraries and the most experienced campaigners. The Romans are nothing if not diligent about writing things down. I studied the campaigns of Gaius Marius, of Sulla, of Caesar. The field experiences of retired legionaries could be heard for the cost of some pitchers of wine in taverns across the empire. I learned whatever I could, however I could. I thought I'd made the right choice. The whole world seems caught up in conquest and expansion—who should be in more demand than an expert strategist who has studied centuries of military history?" He sighed deeply and took a sip of his wine.

"But?" Melchior invited him to continue.

"But I didn't realize the importance of other factors. Rome and its army are the power in the west, and both are brimming with ambitious young Romans eager to make a name for themselves. For them, military success is the avenue to both financial security and political power, and they're not going to yield an inch of advantage to some foreigner, no matter how well educated."

"You'd think they'd listen to a son of the only people to ever defeat Alexander," Melchior observed.

Gaspar chuckled darkly. "You'd think, wouldn't you? But to most Romans, anything east of Dalmatia is 'Greek', and anything east of the Euphrates is 'Parthian', and that's where their interest ends. The names Mithradates and Carrhae still loom too large in the Roman mind. Even trying to get them to understand about lands further east is futile."

"Do you think your youth worked against you?"

Gaspar shrugged. "Alexander had conquered Persia when he was younger than I am now. I may not be an Alexander, but I'm more able than many of the men I saw in command of legions."

"So, you had no success?" Melchior asked.

"Oh, I had some. A senior tribune I met in Hispania engaged me to help plan his campaign against some guerrillas. He was so pleased with my work that he commended me to a prefect in Gaul. I helped the prefect overhaul the dispositions of his entire force, enabling him to cover more territory with fewer men. But when the commendation arrived from Rome, my contribution went unacknowledged, though I know the prefect had mentioned me warmly in his reports. I was paid well, and given helpful letters of introduction, but it was becoming clear: I would never be more than a useful foreigner, excluded from the inner circles of power."

"That must have been disappointing," Melchior said sympathetically.

"Somewhat," Gaspar shrugged. "But not so much as I'd thought. After a few years inside their operations, I'd become a bit disillusioned with Rome. Given my choice of fields, it was the sensible path for me to take, but the reality didn't match the image."

"How so?"

Gaspar pondered a bit before responding. "It's hard to explain. To the Romans, everything's about Rome—an understandable attitude, given what they've achieved. So long as the peace holds so the revenues keep flowing, they worry about nothing else. But those of us who have studied other times and places and peoples can see that the iron might of Rome is not so strong as the Romans believe. Oh, it's plenty strong in Italy, and Gaul, and Hispania, and Africa. But in Anatolia and the Levant, and even Egypt—wherever they've subscribed to Antony's strategy of using client kings—the quality of the iron degrades. Petty kings are happy to use the legions to secure their thrones, and will rally to the Eagles if called, but they aren't interested in aggrandizing Rome. They may swear the oaths and honor any visiting Roman dignitaries, but in their own courts they point out that the Roman military learned at the feet of the

Greek, and that the greatest Roman general would be no match for Alexander. In private, the name Mithradates is held more in honor than in contempt."

"It sounds like you speak from personal experience," Melchior observed.

"In this case, yes. Despairing of achieving my goals among the Romans, I drifted east. I found a position assisting the general of one of the kingdoms of Asia. Despite the fact that the king wouldn't properly fund or equip his army, I helped the general plan and execute a campaign to drive back an aggressive neighbor who'd been harassing the kingdom for generations. The defeat cost the neighboring king his throne, and his successor was willing to negotiate a settlement to the longstanding disagreements. Resolving that problem earned the general an estate and a welcome retirement. He recommended to his successor that I be retained as a strategic advisor, but the successor was a young court noble who wanted one of his drinking buddies to have the job. So I was decorated, paid off, and shown the borders."

"Is that where you picked up your retainers?" Melchior asked.

"A couple of them. Gordias and Keos decided to try their luck with me instead of staying under the new general. Tetius has been with me since Gaul." Gaspar sighed heavily and took another drink. "I just hope they haven't bet on the wrong horse."

"What are your plans now?"

"That's the question, isn't it? With Rome a dead end for me, I could bounce around from one petty Greek kingdom to another. Or I could look to Parthia, the second largest empire in the world. Or I could go home, and try my luck with some raj or *kshatrapa* there. At the moment, I'm not certain what I'll do."

"So that's what brought you here? You're on the route home?"

"That, plus the fact that the summer is ending, so the Parthian Imperial court will soon return from Ecbatana in the mountains to Seleucia on Eulaeus down there in the valley. Perhaps I can make some contacts at court. But mostly it was the draw of this place, the hope that you were still alive and in residence. The years I spent here were the best of my life, and I was hoping that even a brief visit would enable me to recapture some of the peace and hope I knew when I dwelt here."

Melchior noticed the bitter edge in Gaspar's voice—an edge that had come far too early for such a young man. "You're welcome for as long as you wish to stay, which I hope will be longer than a brief visit. It sounds like you need some rest."

"Rest—yes," Gaspar confirmed. "That would be welcome. But enough of me—how have you been? Am I correct in guessing that you're no longer taking students?"

Melchior sighed. "You are. I sent my last student off four years ago. Part of me misses teaching, but part of me was growing weary of it. I certainly didn't need the income any more. I'd put away enough for the rest of my life, and there are advantages to being a magus living just up the hill from the winter capital. Some noble or courtier is always wanting a horoscope cast or a dream interpreted, and is willing to pay for it. Other than that, I've mostly busied myself with managing the estate. That's enough for me at this point in life." Melchior sighed. "But some days I wonder if I didn't stop teaching too early."

Gaspar looked at his old friend and mentor with concern of his own. Melchior's speech was tinged with dusty flatness, with weary resignation that hadn't been there before. Gaspar remembered the verve and enthusiasm of years ago, the voice of a wise teacher excited to introduce his students to wisdom and knowledge. Little of that seemed to remain, and Gaspar wondered what had changed. "Why do you wonder that?" he asked.

Melchior sighed again. "Sometimes I think it might have been good for these old gray hairs to interact with youth and enthusiasm, if only to keep them youthful. Certainly it grew tiresome to go over the same lessons again and again, and to deal with the same discipline matters, but occasionally there came a student with such a teachable mind, with such love and appreciation of knowledge, that it was like getting a bit of my youth back. I could once again taste the hope, the excitement, the wonder of my younger years. You were such a student. Now all I have to look forward to is the steward's reports on how much milk the goats are giving, or how the fruit harvest is shaping up."

"But, don't you have—", Gaspar began, but they were interrupted by a messenger at the doorway.

"Pardon, my lords, but there is a visitor at the gate. He asked for admittance and the chance to see you. He claims to be an old student."

"Ah," said Melchior. "Is he alone?"

"No, my lord. He has a servant, and they were both mounted. He's no beggar. We've invited him in and are hosting him in the guard house. We've attended to their horses, per your instructions."

"Very well. An old student, eh? Perhaps a classmate of yours, Gaspar? We will come greet this visitor. Bid him welcome, and tell him to meet us in the garden. If he is an old student, he will remember the way."

"As you wish, my lord," the servant bowed and whisked away while the two men got to their feet and followed.

"Well," said Melchior. "I wonder what fate would bring two of my former students to my door on the same day?"

"If it is indeed one of your former students," Gaspar cautioned.

"Oh, I don't doubt that," Melchior replied. "I get many visitors at my gate for many reasons, and the guards know how to deal with all types. The only ones who ever claim to be former students are the former students. The only question is whether it's a former student I wish to see."

By now they were entering the garden, which was glowing in the late afternoon light. They turned along the long pool and saw, approaching from the far end, a tall dark man dressed in the colorful draping robes of the hotter climes—Sheba, perhaps, or Nubia, thought Gaspar. The man broke into a broad grin and hurried his pace, while Melchior slowed almost to a stop.

"By the stars and planets," he whispered. "This is a day of good omen."

"Melchior!" boomed the man in a voice that rose from the bottom of his chest.

"Blessed be this day, whose sunrise brought me one old friend and whose sunset has brought me another!" cried Melchior, embracing the man warmly and kissing him in the Persian style. "It has been too many years!"

"Far too many," the man agreed, then turned to Gaspar. "But who is our friend?"

"Another old student, though one who followed you by many years," Melchior explained. "May I present Gudpharasa? My old friend and student Bithisarea."

The men bowed deeply to one another. "In deference to local pronunciation abilities, I normally go by Gaspar."

"Ah," the man smiled. "For similar reasons, in these lands I go by Balthazar."

ACQUAINTANCE

The next morning found the three men strolling in the quiet cool of the garden. The evening before they'd spent getting acquainted, or reacquainted. Balthazar had studied under Melchior some years prior to Gaspar's arrival, and was even more widely traveled. Gaspar had warmed to the man's expansiveness and ebullience, but suspected he had depths of experience and wisdom as well. But they'd shortened the evening to allow the weary travelers their rest, and had broken their fast at dawn in order to spend a leisurely morning together.

"Your garden, always a haven of peace and calm," Balthazar said as they wandered beneath the orange trees. "How many hours I spent here, trying to memorize the star names or the records of kings!"

"And how good it is to have you back," Melchior added. "Tell me, old friend, what brings you to my door? And how goes your search?"

"The two questions are connected—which reminds me, I have a gift for you. I'll fetch it from my room presently. But as to your second question, about my search—"

"For what are you searching?" Gaspar asked.

"For what? Truth. Purity. Order. Constancy." Balthazar explained with a smile and a nod toward Melchior. "A search that springs from a discussion which has been going on for decades, thanks to my wise teacher. We know that there is order

15

in the spheres of the heavens. The stars and planets step their dance with regularity and harmony. The sun rises over that hill, at this hour, on this day, to be greeted by..." He glanced at Melchior.

"Virgo," Melchior confirmed.

"Virgo," Balthazar continued. "As anyone who knows the movement of the heavens can predict. Those who watched the heavenly bodies a thousand, or two thousand, years ago could foresee their future placement with such accuracy that we can rely upon their predictions to this day. Scholars a thousand, or two thousand, years hence will observe the same. It is in the heavens that we find the perfect, the unchanging, the incorruptible. It is only on this earth, beneath the sphere of the moon, that we find corruption and decay and imperfection. We men strive to do things, but our doings go awry. We seek to know, but our knowledge is oft mistaken or imperfect. We seek to build, but our works crumble in our hands. In this sphere of earth, everything is tainted with corruption."

"That's certainly true," Gaspar acknowledged, recognizing this as the usual outlook of mages and philosophers.

"I've always striven to draw closer to that heavenly perfection and, perchance through me in some small way, draw that perfection closer to the earth. With guidance from our master," Balthazar gave a slight bow to Melchior. "I have sought in the realm of religion and spiritual inquiry. For where do our souls reach for the transcendent more than in the ecstasy of worship or the serenity of contemplation? So I've sought out as many sects and schools as I could, plunging into their rites and teachings, embracing enlightenment wherever I could find it. My travels have taken me from Karnak to Ephesus to Babylon to Rome. I have bathed in bull's blood and learned the Seven Names of Mithras and dined at Cybele's table and danced the Bacchanalia, searching, always searching, for the light of the divine in man."

Though Gaspar didn't doubt Balthazar's sincerity, there seemed an element of recitation in his account, as if he was trying to justify himself. But still, his words made Gaspar ponder.

"I suppose, put like that, my own travels could be considered a search—a search for order and harmony, for permanence and glory," Gaspar said.

"Ah, that sounds promising," Balthazar replied. "And where have you been searching?"

"In the realm of the military, and of civil order," Gaspar explained. To his annoyance Balthazar burst into laughter.

"I see. And how much order and harmony have you found among the camp latrines and ambitious officers and greedy governors and grasping councilmen?"

"About as much as you have found among the conniving priests and lecherous temple attendants and greedy acolytes," Gaspar replied with some sharpness.

"Ah," Balthazar paused. "I—I see what you mean."

"I did see all those things, more than I wanted," Gaspar continued. "But I have also seen the centuries arrayed in the morning sunlight, responding smartly to their orders. I've seen dedicated men work endless days against impossible odds to build cities and write laws, trying to impose regularity and justice on chaos, in hopes that their children and grandchildren might know peace and prosperity. Tell me that isn't reaching for order and constancy."

"No, no, I would claim no such thing," Balthazar said clumsily. "I...I see your point." An awkward silence fell for a minute before he spoke again. "And what of you, master? How goes your search?"

Gaspar looked at Melchior with curiosity. This seemed another reference to a long-running conversation, but he'd never heard Melchior refer to any kind of search. He wondered what this was about.

Gaspar was doomed to disappointment. Most uncharacteristically, Melchior stumbled and stammered a few things about slowing down in his old age and having many distractions. As it became embarrassingly clear that he was finding the question difficult, Balthazar distracted him by suddenly remembering his gift and bustling off to fetch it. Gaspar and Melchior chatted about what a unique character the big Arab was until he returned grinning, a cloth-wrapped bundle beneath his arm. He waved them over to a bench as he unwrapped an inlaid sandalwood box. With some ceremony he slid the top off the box, extracted a parchment-wrapped cylinder, and presented it to Melchior as if it was a scepter.

"Thank you, my lord," Melchior bowed as he slipped the thing out of its sheath. It was a tightly wrapped scroll.

"A small token of my appreciation for your years of mentoring, and your service to the world through your wisdom," Balthazar replied.

Gaspar raised his eyebrows. If this was a small token of Balthazar's esteem, he wondered what a large token would look like. That box alone was worth a month's pay, and from the calligraphy on the scroll which Melchior was now unrolling, those had been penned by experienced scribes, works of both scholarship and art. Any one of them would be worth a fortune, and there looked to be five. Melchior, an old hand with precious scrolls, was handling the volume with due reverence.

"This," Balthazar announced with pride. "Is a volume of the sacred writings of the Jews: the Five Books, what they call *Torah.*"

"But—it's in Greek," Melchior replied in amazement. "I understood that the Jews were reluctant to put their sacred writings into anything but their ancient Hebrew."

"Perhaps here in the East," Balthazar said. "But around the Mediterranean there are more Greek-speaking Jews. There have been various accounts as to why and how the translation was made, some involving Ptolemy, prisons, and seventy-two scholars, but there it is. Knowing your love of all works of wisdom, I thought it would be a worthy addition to your library."

Gaspar almost rocked back. 'Worthy addition' was a gross understatement—this was a kingly gift. Melchior clearly understood this as well. He was sitting down on the bench, his hands trembling, and seemed to be having trouble breathing, much less speaking.

"My…my lord, words escape me," Melchior finally choked out. "This is—my heavens."

"The gift is well given, my lord," Gaspar said with a bow to Balthazar.

"But a minor repayment of the incalculable debt which I— which all your students—owe you," Balthazar included Gaspar with a sweep of his hand. Gaspar was grateful for the gracious inclusion, as well as a little conscious of the fact that he'd shown up at the gate empty-handed. But that didn't seem to matter. After Melchior had regained his composure, they examined and discussed the precious scrolls, then made their way to the library to find a suitably honorable spot for them. That kept them busy looking over and discussing matters literary until lunchtime, after which Melchior begged the old man's privilege of an afternoon nap and retired—though Gaspar noticed that he took one of his new scrolls with him.

The week that followed was relaxing and refreshing for all. The worst heat of summer was passing and the equinox was approaching. Captain Tigranes often took the estate guard out for training to restore the edge to their skills after the summer's lethargy, and was happy to take Gaspar's men with them. Sometimes Gaspar and Balthazar would ride along, which Tigranes appreciated, since Gaspar was never short of observations and advice. For his part, Gaspar appreciated how seriously Tigranes took his duties. Far from being just liveried showpieces decorating the estate, the guards were expected to be proficient with the short sword, spear, and javelin when afoot, and the lance and bow on horseback. Gaspar and his men were able to teach them some new maneuvers straight from Roman tactics, and Tigranes made certain everyone was proficient at mounted archery, especially the infamous Parthian shot, the aft-facing draw from the back of a running horse. Gaspar was particularly glad to see his men master that.

"They seem to be catching on quite well, even our odd additions," Balthazar commented one day as the two lords stood off watching the guards go through their paces.

"Soldiers have a common language," Gaspar explained. "A good one can be taken from anywhere, put anywhere, and work well enough to fight."

"Good thing, too, for your Roman doesn't speak much of the local tongue."

"Tetius?" Gaspar chuckled. "No, he doesn't even have any Aramaic, much less Persian. It's the Roman outlook—they figure that eventually the whole world will be speaking Latin, so they're just waiting for everyone else to come around. He has a smattering of Greek, though, which means he can get by."

"I remember wondering about that when I first came here, but it was one of the smartest things the master ever did: requiring everyone to speak only Greek within his walls. Even the scullery boy got an education," Balthazar said. Then he cleared his throat and continued in a more subdued voice. "My lord, I wish to apologize for laughing at you on our first morning here. If there's one thing I should have learned over the years, it's not to laugh at a man, and especially not to laugh at that which he holds most dear. I dealt ill with you, and I'm sorry."

Gaspar smiled. "In that case, I should apologize for my response. The truth is, your comments hit close enough to sting. Yes, I have seen order and purpose and noble intent among magistrates and generals—but it is rare, and far too often eclipsed by self-serving men using those positions for their own advancement rather than the common good."

"It's the way of the world," Balthazar replied.

"I know, but it's so—frustrating," Gaspar said. "Many of them have the potential for greatness, but lack the vision to realize it. They busy themselves with lining their pockets and playing petty tyrant when they could be a Caesar or an Alexander."

"Is that your hope? To someday be an Alexander?"

"Perhaps a Chandragupta," Gaspar replied. "I wish for the vision of one of the great ones, though I doubt my destiny will put me in such a place. I know my limits. I seek not so much the command for myself as a noble captain to follow, a proper general. We are men and serve we must; the best thing we can hope for is to find a true master and serve him well. Even the greatest understand this—in fact, I think it the key to their greatness. It is said that Julius Caesar, for all his self-aggrandizement, never lost sight of the fact that he served Rome. It is also said that his men loved him because he never forgot that he served them as well."

"So that, then, is your search?" Balthazar asked. "To serve a noble general who serves his people?"

"You could put it that way, though I had not thought of it in terms of a search," Gaspar admitted. "It's getting discouraging. I've served under generals who wanted to be emperors and captains who wanted to be kings, but nobody can see beyond their noses. I begin to despair that my ideal can be found on this earth."

Balthazar sighed and nodded. "I can sing that tune too well. Noble as my rhetoric may be, I have seen so many things in my long travels that confirmed your response. I know there is purity and truth among the stars, but I'm becoming discouraged as to whether it can ever be found among men. I began my search certain that the way of transcendence was the path to finding that purity and truth. Call it what you will—true worship, pure devotion, enlightenment, the metaphysical—I was sure that this would lead me, however circuitously, to truth. But I have seen the same thing that you have, though in different arenas. Priests who are the model of devout speech and behavior in public, but in private are cynical and mocking about their rites. Temples that are, for all purposes, brothels. Partisans almost coming to blows over metaphysical nuance in the midst of decay and depravity. Truthfully, I was once so desperate for purity and integrity that I paid to dine with a temple virgin."

"A Vestal?" Gaspar asked.

"No," Balthazar chuckled. "The Romans wouldn't let a dark-skinned foreigner near their precious Vestals. This was a temple virgin of another goddess. Most cults have a place for them in their traditions, even if there are no active devotees. I even had her bathe my hands."

"Bathe your hands?"

"A ritual of that cult. Having a virgin wash your hands with freshly caught rainwater into a silver basin by moonlight is supposed to wash away your sins and offenses."

"Did it work?" Gaspar asked.

"For the temple fee I paid for the rite, it better have," Balthazar said, looking at his hands. "But there was nothing remarkable about the virgin. Plain face, sad eyes. We spoke of common matters. She was hoping for a tip. The temple whores get all of those, while all she got was an allowance and a special place at certain ceremonies.

"That's one instance. I could give you dozens more. Like you searching for your noble general to serve, I have searched for purity and true devotion. And, like you, I have come up empty-handed."

"So far," Gaspar added.

"So far," Balthazar echoed.

"If it would not betray any trusts," Gaspar said cautiously. "You spoke to the master of his search, but he seemed reluctant to respond. For what is he searching, if it may be told?"

"Oh, that," Balthazar waved a dismissive hand. "Nothing secret, and no surprise to anyone who knows him. He searches for true wisdom—the clear message of the gods, or the universe, or the Logos, or whatever you wish to call it."

"Oh, yes," Gaspar nodded. "The love that has driven him as long as I've known him, the love he's tried to pass along to every student who has come through his doors. But why would he not wish to speak of that? I'd think it would be the first thing he'd want to talk about."

"So would I," Balthazar replied gravely. "And the fact that he's so reticent to discuss what was once his most driving passion is not the least of what concerns me about him."

"What do you mean?" Gaspar asked, sensing that he already knew some of the answer.

"Have you not sensed it? His sluggishness, his lack of verve? The dullness of his speech? He used to join us in conversations that lasted far into the night, bubbling with excitement and joy, pursuing the truth of whatever we were discussing. Now he speaks of the crops, and the fish in his pond."

"Well, he is getting older," Gaspar offered.

"That's the excuse he presents, though he's just over three score years. He says he stopped taking students because he was growing older, but I'm beginning to think it might be the other way around."

"What?" Gaspar asked. "That he's getting older because he stopped taking students?"

"Perhaps. He never took students for income, particularly toward the last few years. He took them in hopes of passing along the vision, creating a few more lovers of truth. Then—he stopped. I wonder what happened."

"Perhaps we can ask indirectly?" Gaspar suggested.

"Do you think we or anyone can weasel something out of the master that he doesn't want to give?" Balthazar asked with a smile. "Still, let's keep our eyes and ears open. I think he wants to talk more than he lets on."

At supper that evening Melchior suggested they meet him before dawn the next morning on the observatory tower. They were going to once again gaze at the heavens under Melchior's tutelage.

CONJUNCTION

"My lord! My lord!" came the lad's voice at his elbow. Gaspar's warrior reflexes jerked him awake, causing him to sit up sharply. The lad backed off with a wary look in his eyes.

"I'm sorry, my lord, but you asked me to wake you at this hour," the lad continued, and Gaspar waved his hand.

"Of course I did, lad—Baba, isn't it?"

"Yes, my lord."

"Thank you. Inform my Lord Melchior that I'll be along presently."

The three scholars met at the base of the observation tower in the chill dark. The night was clear as only mountain nights can be, and the sky was a carpet of stars. They began the long climb up the tower steps, letting Melchior lead at his trudging pace. Gaspar remembered racing other students up these steps; now his knee was starting to twinge from the fall he'd taken during that patrol in Hispania. From Balthazar's labored breathing, Gaspar suspected the big Arab hadn't been doing much climbing either in recent years.

At last they emerged onto the broad, flat roof atop the tower. There was only a knee-high wall around the edge, a feature which both fascinated and terrified young students. The platform could hold two dozen people easily, and had no towers or spindles to hinder the view. The tower's height just cleared the shoulder of the mountain against which the estate nestled, so the view was unencumbered from horizon to horizon.

The eastern sky was beginning to lighten, signaling that their observation time was short, but there was still plenty of night remaining. The men read the sky with practiced eyes, spotting familiar stars and planets.

After some while of enjoying the morning quiet and the sky's familiar beauty, Melchior said, "My lords, I appreciate your humoring an old man's request for a pre-dawn sky reading. I have a particular conjunction I wish to point out. It is unique in my lifetime, and I thought it might interest you." He pointed to the east, where the dawn was now lightning the horizon sufficiently to overpower the dimmer stars. But the stars he indicated were right above the horizon, having risen just ahead of the sun, and were still clearly visible.

"Ah, our old friend Leo," Balthazar murmured, tilting his head a little to get a better angle on the magnificent constellation.

"Yes. You'll notice that right by Regulus—whom the Greeks call Basilicusus—he has an additional member," Melchior pointed.

Intrigued, Gaspar and Balthazar peered more closely. The placement of a planet within a constellation was always fraught with significance, especially when one examined which stars the planet approached.

"Is that—Jupiter?" Gaspar asked.

"Yes, to use his Roman name. Zeus to the Greeks and Marduk to the Babylonians," Melchior confirmed.

"I've never seen him so close to Basilicusus," Balthazar said. "He's almost occulting him."

"Oh, it's much more than that," Melchior said. "He's closely passed Regulus twice already, and according to my calculations will do so once more before continuing his passage."

The two younger men turned and gazed at Melchior in wonder. Alone among the heavenly bodies, the five planets did not follow straight paths across the sky. For reasons known only to the heavens, they occasionally looped—stopping in their courses, moving backwards for a while, then stopping again before returning to their forward movement. When and where these reversals took place, and in proximity to which other heavenly bodies, were matters of high interest to those who watched the skies.

"So Jupiter is saluting Regulus not once, but thrice?" Gaspar asked.

"In Leo," Balthazar added. "The King Planet joins the King Star within the figure of the King of Beasts. Master, have you ever seen anything like this?"

"Twice in my life I have seen Jupiter draw within five degrees of Regulus, but never have I seen him linger this close for this long," Melchior admitted. The advancing dawn was now lightening the eastern sky significantly, but the two bright bodies were still plainly visible.

"What follows?" Balthazar asked. When trying to decipher the heavens, sometimes the next stars or constellations in procession would shed interpretive light on some astral event.

"See for yourselves," Melchior invited them, pointing to the glowing east. They stood in silence for a while as enough stars cleared the horizon to make the constellation visible. They were dimming in the waxing sunlight, but could still be seen.

"Virgo," Balthazar confirmed. "Virgo, with the sun rising into her."

"Virgo," Gaspar muttered. "What could that mean?"

The first edge of the sun's orb broke the horizon. "My lords, shall we break our fast?" Melchior asked, gesturing them down the steps to where the morning repast was laid out in an intimate little room just off the main dining area. They enjoyed the fruits and delicate sweet cakes as they discussed what they had seen.

"I hope you can see why I invited you up for one last lesson," Melchior said. "I have been watching that since earlier this year, when I first noticed Jupiter lingering near Regulus."

"Whenever a planet loops like that, the heavens are trying to tell us something," Gaspar said. "I wonder what it is?"

"Why, shouldn't it be obvious?" Balthazar answered. "The King Planet hailing the King Star? Repeatedly? I'm not sure what the lion might mean, unless it's simply the King of Beasts. The advent of some great king, to be sure! A king so great that even the skies hail his arrival."

"Aye, but which king?" Gaspar replied. "To what people? Will Rome again have a king? Despite their republican affectations, their emperors may as well be kings. Will another Alexander arise among the Greeks? Or another Darius among the Persians? And what might Virgo have to do with it all? A reference to the Vestals, perhaps? But no, Rome's symbol is the eagle, not the lion. A resurgent Carthage?" Gaspar's musings descended into muttering while Balthazar looked to Melchior, who had been largely silent through this spirited exchange.

"What think you, master? Surely you have some consideration, some interpretation, of these signs?"

Melchior sighed, looking older and wearier than his friends had ever seen him. He seemed to begin to speak, then paused and bowed his head.

"You asked, some days ago, how my search was faring. I found it difficult to respond then, and I still find it difficult, but I owe you an answer. This is it, though it weighs on my heart to say it: in truth, I feel that my search has come to a futile end, and I pursue it no longer. I don't know any answers, and I'm not sure there are any to find, any more than I know that there is meaning to the movements of the heavens like we saw this morning."

The two younger lords looked at each other in shock. Shaken as their outlooks had been by their own experiences, they'd always held on to the hope offered by their master's undaunted search for truth. Now, it seemed, he had given up the quest.

"But master," Gaspar offered hesitantly. "Such a momentous event—surely it signifies something."

"What, though?" Melchior replied. "Certainly it is unusual, unique in my lifetime, but is it saying anything? And if so, what? What being would so write in the skies? And having done so, would he then make what he had written known to men? Seers from Hispania to the land of the Hind are reading what the skies are writing, and all will come up with their own interpretations, and all will be accounted wisdom, even though they might not agree, or may even contradict. These interpretations will undoubtedly flatter their patrons, or advance their own interests, but will bear little relation to the truth.

"But what is the truth? What might these omens signify? I once thought that even if the meaning was obscured, it could ultimately be discerned, if only with difficulty. But now—now I wonder if there is any meaning or pattern at all. Do the gods speak to men? If so, why is their speech so obscure? Why communicate with signs and omens that are so difficult to interpret? Why not speak plainly?"

Melchior fell silent, gazing at his hands, while his two friends looked at him and each other in stunned silence.

"This—this is quite a change, master," Balthazar said at last.

"I know it must be, especially to you two, who were nurtured in the love of wisdom in this very house. I fear…" Melchior sighed. "I fear that is why I did not give your unspeakably generous gift the thanks it richly deserved. For decades now friends have been bringing me histories and wisdom writings from many peoples, and for years I have welcomed them as more resources for my search.

"But it was—well, several years ago now when some friends brought me a rare treasure: several ancient scrolls that had been found in a chest in Ecbatana. They dated back to the days of the Persian empire, court records and the like. As antiquities they were priceless, badly faded but still legible, written in an older Persian that only I could read.

"Of course, these records contained various horoscopes and interpretations which had been prepared for the emperor and his officials. At first I poured through them with great excitement, seeking to understand their interpretive principles. I had centuries of material, reaching back to the empire's earliest days, some of it written by legendary magi. All their experience, all their insights, lay open to me.

"It was while I was examining these scrolls that it occurred to me: not one of these predictions foretold the coming of Alexander. These were the most renowned seers in the world, supposedly the very mouthpieces of the gods, specifically charged—and handsomely paid—to guide the emperors in the running of the empire. Yet not one of them foresaw the coming of the mightiest general in history. Thousands upon thousands of lines of predictions and interpretations, but not one that spoke of the most significant event the empire would face!

"That was what got me thinking and questioning. I was so eager to study the interpretive principles of the old Persian school, yet the very outcome proved them futile. What good is it to diligently read the skies and omens so you can advise the emperor on which official to elevate to which satrapy, or which sacrifices to offer before the spring planting, when your art cannot foresee the coming of the conqueror who will destroy your empire? Yet not one of them saw him coming! Centuries of records, thousands of oracles, yet not one foretold him! Not one!"

"One did," Balthazar said quietly.

Gaspar looked at him as Melchior's head snapped up.

"Who?" Melchior asked. "Which Persian sage spoke of the coming of Alexander? I have searched the records—"

"You wouldn't find him in those records, or perhaps in any Persian court records. He wasn't Persian. His name was Bel'Tshazzar.

"Chaldean, then?" Melchior asked.

"Actually, no," Balthazar explained. "He had a Babylonian name, and worked for the Babylonians before Babylon fell to Darius, after which he worked for the Persians. But he was a Jew, one of the exiles who was captured in Judah by Nebuchadnezzar. His native name was Dani'el."

"And he foresaw the coming of Alexander?"

"Apparently not only that, but the fall of Babylon, the rise of Persia, the coming of Alexander and the division of his kingdom, and the rise of Rome as well."

"Really?" Melchior asked skeptically. "Where did you learn of this gifted seer?"

"At a school in Alexandria," Balthazar said. "Some scholars began discussing whether the Roman Empire would last for a thousand years, or if it was truly the final empire the world would ever know, the pinnacle of civilization. A Jewish scholar nearby began laughing at them, saying that Rome would fall like all the other empires of men. They began mocking him and asking who on the world stage could possibly contend with Rome, and he said it didn't matter. He pointed out all the great empires of the past, and that they'd all fallen—some very quickly— and that this Bel'Tshazzar had predicted all of it centuries ago. He also said that Bel'Tshazzar had foreseen the fall of Rome, which didn't go over well with the man who'd been arguing that Rome was the last empire the world would ever see."

Melchior eyed Balthazar with skepticism. "Did this Jewish scholar say which methods this Bel'Tshazzar used? Did he read the skies? Interpret entrails?"

"Dreams and visions, apparently, my lord. He didn't have any methods, attributing everything to his god, who not only sent the visions but revealed their meaning."

"Ah. And I imagine this Jewish god speaks only to his Jewish people?" Melchior asked.

"I didn't get into much detail with the scholar, but I understand that the first dream was sent to the emperor of Babylon himself. He could not understand it, and neither did his seers, but this Bel'Tshazzar provided the interpretation."

"Well," Melchior said, rubbing his beard. Gaspar could sense the struggle within him—the rekindling of hope and curiosity warring with weariness and despair. "All very well, I suppose, but to what far corner of the earth would one have to travel to find the works of this Bel'Tshazzar? And what language would one have to learn?"

"My understanding from this Jewish scholar," Balthazar explained. "Is that you'd have to go right down the hill, where you could probably speak either Greek or Aramaic, since everyone does down there."

"Down the hill? To Seleucia?"

"Yes. You recall its ancient name."

"Of course—Susa."

"Apparently that is where this Bel'Tshazzar ended his days, and did much of his writing. His tomb is there, as is a school of scholars who study his works. Both Jews and Persians, I understand," Balthazar said.

Melchior sat staring at Balthazar, his lips moving silently. Gaspar noticed that he was clutching the table edge so tightly that his knuckles were white. "Tigranes," he finally murmured. "Tigranes would know about this." He beckoned a servant over and sent him to fetch Tigranes.

"What would Tigranes know about this?" Balthazar asked.

"He's a Jew. About every month he goes down to Seleucia with a few other members of the household who are Jews to celebrate their rituals. All the members of that community know one another—he would know of any scholars there."

"Tigranes doesn't sound like a Jewish name," Gaspar observed.

"Most Jews have two names, some have more," Balthazar explained. "One name in their ancestral Hebrew, and also typically a Greek name, and sometimes another—perhaps Roman or Egyptian."

"You summoned, my lord?" Tigranes asked as he entered the room and bowed to the scholars. He was in riding gear, so had probably been preparing to drill the men this morning.

"Yes, Captain," Melchior said. "Balthazar tells me that there is a community of scholars down in Seleucia who study the work of one of your ancient seers, one Bel'Tshazzar."

"Yes, my lord," Tigranes confirmed. "The prophet whom we call Dani'el."

"Then you have heard of this mage?" Melchior asked, his voice hopeful. "And these scholars?"

"Of course, my lord. My uncle Sh'mon is one of them. I just spoke with him two weeks ago."

"Really?" There was no hiding the excitement in Melchior's voice. "Do you think that he would be willing to consult with us on the teachings of this—this Dani'el?"

"He would be honored, my lord," Tigranes bowed. "I'm certain that some of his Persian colleagues would be happy to come as well. Dani'el is accounted a seer of Jew and Persian alike. His are not secret writings, but open to all who seek the truth."

"All who seek the truth," muttered Melchior. "Yes, let us arrange this as quickly as we can."

QUEST

Gaspar strolled through the garden in the morning cool, feeling restless. As tranquil as the estate was, and as much as he enjoyed the company, he was beginning to itch to be back in the saddle, to see other places and horizons.

Yes, but where?

At Melchior's request, Gaspar and Balthazar had wintered at the estate, enjoying the seasonal cool and serene environs. Even as spring had passed, their host had begged them to stay, hinting at great things to come, though remaining vague as to what they might be. But now summer was nearing, with the solstice just days away, and Gaspar was starting to crave another mission.

Gaspar and Balthazar speculated that whatever Melchior alluded to had something to do with his near-constant consultations with the scholars of Seleucia on Eulaeus, or Susa on Ulai to use the ancient name. Hardly a day went by that Melchior didn't rebuke himself for the years he had lost by not learning of this school earlier. He had used Seleucia and its merchants as a trading point, a place where he could purchase ancient texts and put out word of what he was searching for. Now he berated himself for never considering the ancient city as a place of learning in its own right.

Melchior seemed to be trying to make up for lost time by hosting Jewish and Persian scholars at the estate, sometimes for weeks at a time. They listened to lectures and held highly technical discussions and engaged in spirited debates far into the night. Sometimes Balthazar would join these sessions, particularly to talk to the Jewish scholars, known as rabbis. Gaspar didn't participate as much, the discussions being just a little too complicated for him, but he was glad to see Melchior regaining some of his old fire. Their lively, truth-seeking mentor had returned. Once again Melchior could be seen walking the halls and grounds at odd hours, lost in thought, muttering to himself, with at least one scroll under his arm. He again spent late nights up on the observation tower, star charts scattered about. Balthazar's gift of the Jewish holy books got heavy use, as did many scholarly books brought up from the school in Seleucia. Melchior seemed determined to make up for his oversight by examining every page of Jewish wisdom he could lay his hands on.

Gaspar didn't know much about the Jews, except for a few mercenary bands he'd encountered. In the martial world they had a reputation for fierce loyalty, scrupulous fairness, unquestioned ability, and curious habits. But that latter was common to Jews everywhere, as Balthazar had explained. Balthazar's studies had brought him into more regular contact with Jews, but even in his circles they were considered oddities. For one thing, they had no pantheon, being obsessive about their One God and His laws, which meant they couldn't worship the gods of whichever city they lived in. Since that worship was the basis of the civic order, that made the Jews suspect in the eyes of some. But on the whole the Jews were an orderly people, so long as you let them live according to their customs and meet to study their laws. There were enclaves of Jews from Hispania to Parthia, and even beyond to the land of the Hind.

In the religious world Jews were largely discounted. Though they made much of their God, the general consensus was that He couldn't be very strong, because the Jews lacked imperial stature or even a land of their own. Oh, some of them still clung to a patch of dusty land in the Levant, all that remained of their ancient homeland. Their holy city was there, and their main temple, but even that was a polite fiction. They occupied their ancestral land at the sufferance of the Romans—and the Greeks before them, and the Persians before them, and the Babylonians before them. The cult of the Egyptian gods was older, and that of the Roman gods was (obviously) more potent. There didn't seem to be much to recommend the singular god of the Jews.

Besides, Balthazar explained, there wasn't much give-and-take between Jewish and non-Jewish religious scholars, with rare exceptions like the school in Seleucia. The Jews didn't see anything they could learn from other religions, and were mortified if anyone tried to identify their God with any other. As a people they obsessed about the covenant they had with their God. This caused them to view people as falling into two camps: those within the covenant, and those outside it. This gave some of them a bit of a snobbish air, which grated on some non-Jewish scholars, who would at times pointedly observe that this covenant didn't seem to be doing the Jews much good, being as they were scattered, diminished, and subjugated. Balthazar, always open to investigating new things, had once looked into what it took to enter this covenant. The rabbi to whom he'd spoken had allowed as how it was likely that Balthazar had some Israelite blood in him somewhere, and as an Arab he'd already undergone the requisite—ah—physical modifications. But the exclusivity had put Balthazar off. Were he in this covenant, he'd no longer be able to visit other temples and shrines, and devotion to any other god was strictly prohibited.

But there was no denying that the Jews were an ancient people, and their store of wisdom was vast. Their glory days had been centuries before the Butchers of Nineveh had risen to terrorize the world, and now all that remained of the Assyrians were moldering ruins while the Jews endured. Four empires had risen, peaked, and fallen since the Jews had first built their temple in Jerusalem, and Rome was the fifth. That Jewish scholar in Alexandria could be forgiven for laughing at the idea that Rome was the final empire, the ultimate government of the world. The Jews had heard that before.

All this Gaspar had gleaned from his discussions with Balthazar, particularly during the long winter nights. He'd also found other ways to pass his time: hunts, rides, drilling his men with every weapon in the estate's armory. They made their way down to Seleucia regularly, which was livelier now that the emperor's court had shown up for the winter season. (Tetius, who had seen the glories of Rome, obviously had an opinion of the Parthian emperor and his court, which he prudently kept to himself.) Gaspar had even picked up a contract to escort a caravan as far as Ctesiphon, which not only earned the men a little money but kept them all sharp. In Ctesiphon Keos had let Gaspar know that he'd had enough of the East, so Gaspar had paid him off and sent him on his way with all good wishes. Gordias and Tetius had elected to stay for now, but Gaspar could tell that they were eager to be back about their chosen work. He needed to either use them or let them go.

This night, Melchior had asked them to a late feast, the main dish of which would be a gazelle which Gaspar had shot on a hunting trip the day before. The cook had made much of this, promising a grand Persian banquet to honor the successful hunt. Gaspar was fairly certain the cook could do better with one of the fattening calves or young sheep of the estate than with the tough carcass of a gamey, stringy gazelle, but old traditions die hard.

To Gaspar's surprise, the feast was just the three of them: himself, Balthazar, and Melchior as unusually exuberant host. Most of the feasts over the recent months had included at least one visiting scholar or rabbi. The table was lavish, every lamp was burning, and the roasted gazelle was brought in to drums and horns, its head set intact on the platter in the classic style. They all shared the beast's brains, Gaspar receiving the honorary hunter's portion, and then partook of the game. Gaspar's already high opinion of the cook rose even higher—he'd done something with the juices, oils, and spices to tenderize the meat and mitigate the gamey flavor.

The wine flowed and the men laughed, enjoying their friendship. But to Gaspar, it seemed that Melchior was especially poised, almost as if he was sitting on some secret that he intended to unveil. Nor was Gaspar wrong. As the feast wound down, Melchior stood and began to speak in an instructional style.

"My dear friends and fellow scholars, I thank you for joining me here tonight, as well as for humoring my requests that you stay with me during these past several months of study and research. Tonight I hope to reward your patience with some amazing results, as well as a challenge worthy of such noble princes as yourselves."

Balthazar and Gaspar exchanged glances, partly in surprise and partly wondering if it was their mentor or the wine that was speaking so grandiosely. Melchior caught the byplay and wagged a not-quite-sober finger at them.

"I am not merely flattering, my friends. When you hear the results of my research, I am sure you will agree.

"To begin: you remember the astral sign we observed last autumn? Marduk—Jupiter— saluting Regulus three times? The King Planet drawing near the King Star? Single conjunctions of those bodies have happened before, but a triple conjunction is unprecedented—it has never been observed. And do not forget that it happened in Leo—that will be important later.

"But what is the meaning of this singular event? Who could say? Thanks to the help of our friend Balthazar," Melchior bowed slightly to his guest. "I began a study, what some might call a digression, into the records of the Jewish seer to the

Persian court known as Bel'Tshazzar. I would remind you that this seer, known to his people as Dani'el, was the only one who not only foresaw the fall of Persia by the hand of Alexander, but the fall of Alexander and the division of his kingdom, and the rise of Rome, as well as—" Suddenly Melchior checked himself. "As well as other things, to which we will return in time.

"It is important to note that Bel'Tshazzar did not ascribe his prophetic accuracy to any interpretive principles or school, but rather to his god. He claimed, frequently and without hesitation, that the visions he was given, and the visions given to others which he interpreted, were sent directly from this god, as was the wisdom to understand them. And since he was a Jew, there is no doubt about which god he meant: the great God, the God-beyond-gods."

"Bah," scoffed Balthazar. "How can the God-beyond-gods be known by mere mortals, or he know of them? Is he not too great for our minds to understand? Is he not too far removed to even know of our affairs, much less concern himself with them? Is that not the reason for the lesser gods of myth and legend, to convey to us the hints and glimmers of that greatness which we cannot directly apprehend?"

"According to the Jews, he makes himself known through covenant and Law," Melchior explained.

"Ah, say the Jews!" Balthazar waved dismissively. "With the Jews he makes his covenant! To the Jews he gives his Law! What of the rest of us?"

"In the writings of their seers, the Jews hint of a day when there will be a covenant offered to all the nations, not just the Jews," Melchior replied. "Bel'Tshazzar was given a vision of one like a son of men—not a son of the gods, mind you, but a son of men—who received from the God-beyond-gods dominion over all peoples and nations. There was also the vision of the Great Mountain, growing from a rock not cut by human hands, that filled the entire earth. That vision was given to the

Babylonian emperor, who was not a Jew! And that was the rock that smashed the feet of the statue—"

"Melchior, please," Gaspar groaned. "Smashing rocks that grow into mountains, sons of men being elevated by gods—if you'd wanted us to follow all this mystical stuff, you shouldn't have given us so much wine!"

"Forgive me," Melchior smiled. "You know how I can get carried away. We can discuss details later. For now, the important thing is that these two visions—the appearance of the son of man in the celestial court and the rock that grew into a mountain that filled the earth—these are connected, possibly even identical, events. Jewish and Persian scholars agree that they refer to the establishment of the world-wide reign of the Great God and the coming of His Champion, whom the Jews call their *Mesiach*, or Anointed One.

"But here's the important thing," Melchior leaned forward, his eyes glittering with excitement. "The visions not only give the events, they give times! The rock that smashes the statue and then grows into the mountain—that happens during the time of the Fourth Empire, which is clearly Rome! And not in the time of Rome's strength, but in the time of her weakness and decadence, when she is polluting her might by mixing it with that of lesser kingdoms!"

"The client-kings of the East?" Gaspar muttered.

"Possibly," Melchior replied. "But in another vision, when a heavenly messenger is sent to explain the meaning to Bel'Tshazzar, the messenger is quite clear about the years: seventy sevens, or four hundred ninety. In Jewish thought the number seven is fraught with significance, relating to covenant, completion, and perfection. The scholars dispute the mystical meaning of the seventy sevens, but they agree on one thing: that is about the number of years between Bel'Tshazzar's time and now."

"Really?" mused Balthazar, clearly captivated. "The heavenly messenger told Bel'Tshazzar the number of years, and now they are up?"

"Yes," Melchior replied. "We cannot be sure of the precise year, because of some confusion of calendars, but if the seventy sevens have even a shred of literal meaning, then this is the time—which coincides with the weakening of the Fourth Kingdom, and its being smashed by the rock that swells to fill the earth."

"And the triple-conjunction of Regulus and Jupiter," added Gaspar.

"In Leo! In Leo!" cried Melchior, nearly dancing with excitement. "There's more! In the Jewish sacred writings, the patriarch Israel names the tribe of Judah as being the Tribe of the Lion, bearing the scepter! And the line of Jewish kings, the line of David, is of the tribe of Judah. The Jews look to that line for their *Mesiach*, their great king."

"Um," Gaspar said hesitantly. "I'm no expert on Jewish history, but I seem to recall that when the Babylonians swept through the land of the Jews, they didn't leave any kings standing. Neither did the Persians. They had satraps, to be sure, but the only king in the Persian domain sat down there in Susa."

"Right you are," Melchior confirmed. "The Jewish scholars apprised me of that. The last king of the line of David who sat in Jerusalem was one Zedek'iah, who was taken captive to Babylon to be imprisoned for rebellion. The line of David was cut off—though there have been numerous hopeful prophecies of that line being revived.

"However, almost two hundred years ago, the Greeks tried to exterminate the Jews," Melchior began, but Balthazar interrupted.

"Did they? Which Greeks? The Ptolomies of Egypt?"

"No, it seems to have been a Seleucid—one Antiochus Epiphanes," Melchior explained.

"Really?" laughed Gaspar. "He of the circle-in-the-sand fame?"

"What's that?" Balthazar asked.

"If it was him—I know it was Antiochus IV, and I think it's the same king," Gaspar replied. "Seems he got designs on Egypt, as the Seleucids had been doing for centuries, and marched down there with an army. But by then Egypt had become Rome's breadbasket, and a Roman senator named Gaius Popillius Laenas was in Egypt to insure the grain kept flowing. This Gaius and his twelve lictors marched out to meet Antiochus and his army."

"That must have been something to see," Balthazar chuckled. "A Roman with twelve lictors facing down a Greek king and his army."

"Apparently it was. The Roman told Antiochus to go home, and handed him a letter detailing what the Romans wanted him to do. Antiochus took the letter, read it, and said that he wanted to think about it. The Roman simply drew a circle in the sand with his staff, right around the king's feet, and said in essence, 'Think about it in there'."

The men burst into laughter. "I presume his time of thought was short," Balthazar said.

"It was. Of course, Antiochus could have taken down the Roman and his lictors, but he couldn't have dealt with the legions that would have followed. So he turned around and went home. At least, that's how they tell it in Rome. The Greeks might tell a different tale."

"I'm sure they would," Melchior said. "Perhaps that was still rankling him, for he dropped a heavy hand on the Jews, pressuring them to abandon their laws and traditions and become good Greeks like everybody else. Apparently some Jews already had, but others resisted to the point of rebellion. They rose up and ultimately defeated the Greeks and drove them from Judea, reestablishing the kingdom."

"Perhaps," Gaspar said. "But only to have Pompey come along and subjugate them again, as he did to all those petty kingdoms."

"True, true, that being the Roman way, at least in the East," Melchior admitted. "The scholars were unclear about recent developments. There apparently has been some scheming, but the important thing is that after centuries of vacancy, there is again a king in Jerusalem. The throne is occupied—just in time for an ancient prophecy to come due, and an unprecedented sign to be seen in the heavens."

Balthazar and Gaspar looked at each other with raised eyebrows. Melchior was right—this was a suspicious number of coincidences. It seemed the old sage had not yet finished, but Balthazar had a question.

"What of Virgo, Melchior? Last autumn Leo was followed by Virgo. Do the writings speak to that?"

"I've not found anything," Melchior replied, shaking his head. "If the procession of Virgo has meaning, it is shrouded. But—", his eyes glittered and he nearly bounced on his feet. "There is one more thing I wish to show you, something that will harmonize all of this."

"What is it?" Gaspar asked, looking around the banquet hall.

"Oh, you'll have to come see. Follow me to the observation tower!"

"The observation tower!" groaned Gaspar. "After a full meal and two pitchers of wine? Melchior, you torturer!" With moans and laughter they levered themselves to their feet and followed Melchior to the tower stairs, where they had a raucous time wobbling their way up the narrow staircase. At the top they made sure to stay well away from the platform edges as they attended Melchior, who was behaving a bit like a performance manager eager to introduce his next act.

"Well, Melchior, we're here," Balthazar said.

"So you are, to be rewarded for your perseverance. My lords, behold." With a theatric wave, Melchior gestured to the western sky. The two men squinted, then nodded appreciatively. "That's certainly noticeable," Balthazar admitted. "What do we have there, exactly?"

In the western sky hung the brightest star any of them had ever seen, far outshining anything around it.

"What is that? A planetary conjunction?" Gaspar asked.

"Precisely," Melchior confirmed. "Our Lord Marduk— Jupiter—who last autumn was saluting Regulus in Leo, has traversed the heavens to come in close conjunction with Ishtar, known in the west as Venus."

"The mother star, associated of old with the Queen of Heaven," Balthazar noted. "And that's the closest conjunction I've ever seen. It's like they're one star."

"Indeed," Melchior agreed. "My lords, you are looking at the brightest object in the heavens, apart from the sun and moon, that any living man has ever seen or will see. The effective joining of the King Star with the Mother Star."

"So—what might that mean?" Gaspar asked.

"I think you can figure that out," Melchior said with a smug smile. "Remember the day we saw Jupiter salute Regulus? Count the months forward to today, when this sign greets us in the heavens."

The men figured for a bit in their wine-fogged haze. "Nine— or nine and a half, or thereabouts," Balthazar finally announced. Melchior nodded in response, saying nothing but raising his eyebrows expectantly. Gaspar caught the hint.

"The time it takes to bring a child to term."

"Very good," Melchior confirmed. "If the heavenly spectacle we saw last autumn heralded the conception of a great king, the conjunction of the King Star and the Mother Star which we see tonight would announce the king's birth for the whole world to see. But particularly for us standing here, near the tomb

of Bel'Tshazzar, notice the direction in which the conjunction
stands."

"Due west," Gaspar observed.

"Directly above the holy city of the Jews—Jerusalem,"
Balthazar continued.

"My lords, I submit to you that this is not wishful thinking,"
Melchior said firmly. "This is not the selective choosing and
interpreting of omens to support a preferred outcome—
something we have all seen far too often. These signs in the
heavens are plain for all to see. When considered with the Jewish
sacred writings, particularly those of Bel'Tshazzar, whose
veracity is confirmed by historical record, they clearly indicate
momentous events. My guess is that a great king has been born,
possibly the great king for whom the Jews have hoped and
waited, the mountain that will fill the earth, the son of man to be
given dominion over all people."

Balthazar and Gaspar gazed in wonder at the two planets
standing so close that they looked like one star, their mentor's
voice filling the clear night.

"My lords, I invite you to join me on a quest, possibly my
last and hopefully my greatest. I wish to see this great king, this
child whom even the stars assemble to honor. I wish to journey
to Jerusalem to do him homage. Will you come with me?"

Standing beneath the hosts of heaven, Balthazar and Gaspar
felt overwhelmed by majesty, as if they were being swept up into
great events far beyond their control. They looked at each other
and nodded.

"We will come," said Balthazar for them both.

ALWENAH

Tigranes looked out over the assembly gathered before the gates of the estate and sighed. His master had been hastening him to get this expedition going, chafing at the three-week delay, but even that had been barely time to assemble the men and materials needed. There were the three lords themselves and their retainers, and the cook and some assistants, and a scribe or two to record things, and a herald fluent in Greek, Latin, and Aramaic. They had to bring sufficient funds to take them there and back, as well as gifts to placate the various lords and dignitaries they were sure to encounter, as well as sufficient protection for the hazardous road. All these people required provision, so they had to bring enough to be able to survive at least a week on the road before needing to reprovision.

Fortunately, Lord Gaspar had been most helpful with Tigranes' end of things, which had been planning for the route itself. They had needed to put some careful consideration into their travel plans. One option was to go down to Seleucia and join up with other travelers transiting this section of road to form a caravan. But Melchior hadn't wanted it to be widely known that he'd be absent from the estate for a long while, and traveling in a caravan always meant moving at the pace of the slowest member. Besides, some caravans were concerned about being joined by parties with too many lances, for fear of treachery along some lonely stretch of road.

47

So they elected to travel as their own group. To do that safely they'd need about three dozen men-at-arms, which meant that Tigranes had to go down to Seleucia to hire about a dozen more guards for escort. The plan was to travel on or near the main northwest road, using it for speed when they could but moving off it from time to time to make their progress unpredictable. Three dozen lances were enough to deter casual bandits but was insufficient to tangle with the more determined tribal bands that could track travelers along the road for miles and then ambush them at dangerous junctures. Enough variation in their route would reduce that risk. There were cities and villages they knew of just far enough off the main road to permit them to rest and reprovision without drawing too much attention to themselves.

They intended to steer clear of major cities like Ctesiphon, not only because entanglements there would slow them down but also because spotters lingered near such places to identify traveling parties like theirs for attack. The first large city they were aiming for was Hatra, well up the Tigris, at which point they would turn west toward Damascus and then south toward Jerusalem. With luck and minimal complications in reprovisioning, they should complete the journey in five months. Melchior had spoken to pilgrims who had made the trip in four months, but Gaspar and Tigranes, who had more experience moving large groups of people, were figuring five.

Gaspar came riding up with his two retainers, looking ready to depart. The men's lances were bundled with some of the other baggage, but they had their swords strapped to one side of their saddles and their bows and quivers on the other.

"For whom are we waiting?" Gaspar asked.

"My Lord Melchior," Tigranes explained. "For all his agitation to be on the road, he has some final words for his chamberlain."

"Well, we could be gone for over a year," Gaspar replied. "Have you seen Baba?"

"I put him on one of the pack camels," Tigranes pointed. "He has a special ability with the beasts, though he's still finding his seat atop them." Like most Parthian lads, Baba could ride as well as he could walk, but it was taking him a while to get used to the swaying height and loping gait of the dromedaries they'd picked up in Seleucia as the primary pack beasts for the journey.

Gaspar grinned. "Once he does, I'll have to see if I can get Balthazar to teach him how to get them galloping. You wouldn't believe it for their size, but those camels can move swiftly when handled properly—a fact that Arab raiders use to make themselves the terror of their neighbors." He trotted off for a word with Baba.

Finally, Melchior came out of the gate, the estate chamberlain close behind still asking a string of questions. As Melchior mounted his horse, Balthazar nudged his Arabian mount over beside him. The small caravan was arrayed along the road while most of the estate's staff lined the wall beside the gate. Sensing the expectation that he'd make a declamation of some sort, Melchior rose in his saddle.

"We begin this journey in hopes of great achievement which history will remember. May the gods look with favor upon our roads and return us safely to this house."

Balthazar smiled. This was a speech pitched more to reassure the hearers than to express Melchior's nuanced theism. Balthazar knew the old mage personally tended to think of God as did the Greek philosophers—all powerful and infinitely distant in his abstract perfection. Melchior also had sympathy for the stern dualism of Zoroaster, so popular here in Persia, with its eternal struggle between good and evil. Yet beneath the detached intellectualism lay a glimmer of hope, a child's hope, that somehow God or the gods cared enough about men to speak to them, to reach out and reassure them they were not alone in the vast, impersonal universe. It was this dim flicker which Balthazar had seen almost extinguished, and which the promise of this expedition had renewed. For the sake of his friend and mentor, Balthazar breathed a quiet prayer to whatever god might be listening that the effort would not be in vain.

From atop his camel, Baba could see his mother and father and sisters clearly. He was the only son, and for that reason Mother had been wary of letting him accompany the journey. But Father, wise Father, had interceded. To see Hatra, and Damascus, and far Jerusalem, and possibly Tyre and Antioch as well—that was the opportunity of a lifetime! Besides, this wouldn't be some slipshod merchant convoy. All three lords were going, with a well-armed escort, including Captain Tigranes. He waved to his family, feeling a thrill of pleasure at his good luck mingling with a pang of homesickness.

"Ready, lad?" asked Lord Gaspar, who was seated on his horse nearby. The caravan was snaking down the road now, and the lead driver was chivvying the first camels into their places in line. Baba was on a camel toward the rear of the convoy, charged with keeping the latter camels in place and notifying the drivers of problems.

"Oh—yes, my lord," Baba answered.

"Just let him have his head," Gaspar assured him. "He'll follow the others by instinct. But if he tries to nose ahead or break out of line, don't be afraid to use the quirt."

"Yes, sir," Baba replied, fingering the stiff leather whip that hung by his saddle. He still felt a little overawed that one of the lords was chatting with him.

"Relax, lad," Lord Gaspar smiled. "The camel has been doing this longer than you have. If you're nervous up there, he'll pick up on it and get unmanageable. Trust his instincts. Give him respect and he'll return it."

"Yes, my lord," Baba said, trying to sound relaxed and confident. "Ah—my lord?"

"Yes, lad?"

"Do you think we'll have any adventures on this journey?"

Gaspar chuckled. "I hope not, lad. This is your first journey away from home, isn't it?"

"Except for trips down to Seleucia, yes, my lord."

"You'll soon learn that traveling is like life—long stretches of dreary monotony punctuated by brief spells of frantic terror. Those brief spells are what you might call 'adventures', if you look back at them many years later, or hear of them happening to someone else. When you're in the middle of them, you want to be anywhere else. On this journey, the most adventure we're likely to see is some bandit raids, though hopefully they'll count our spears and think better of it. If by some ill chance adventure finds us, remember to do your duty. That's what is expected of a man."

"I—I will, sir," Baba assured him.

"Good lad," Lord Gaspar said, then spurred his horse to ride up to where his men were. Baba looked after him in awe. It was rumored among the guards that Lord Gaspar had ridden with the Roman Legions, and had visited Africa and Rome and even far Gaul, which was on the other side of the world! Yet he took the time to instruct Baba in the proper handling of camels! Baba settled back in the saddle and tried not to be nervous as the caravan wound down the river road toward the valley.

A straight run up the main road to Ctesiphon would take about three weeks, but since they wanted to avoid that city, they occasionally took side roads through valleys that paralleled the main road. This also enabled them to purchase their provisions directly from farmers and herders, thus avoiding the outrageous markups charged by the merchants along the more traveled ways. As they drew closer to Ctesiphon and were more often delayed by other caravans, they decided to follow a slightly longer detour that would take them north through some valleys which Gaspar knew. There was a city there, Lur Dokis, where they could rest a few days, reprovision properly, and then angle back down to rejoin the main road well west of Ctesiphon.

Gaspar led the way along the narrow mountain roads, finally coming over the saddle of a pass shortly after noon on their second day off the main road.

"Looks well-tended," Tigranes observed to Gaspar as they looked down on the fields and meadows carpeting the valley below.

"Yes. The people of Lur Dokis are peaceful and industrious," Gaspar replied, but something within him was sounding an alarm. The tidy fields, near to ripening in the summer sun, were empty of people. And where were the flocks and shepherds that should be scattered across the meadows?

"Where is the city?" Tigranes asked.

"Beyond that shoulder of rock," Gaspar pointed. "An hour's riding should bring it into view."

"What's that smudge in the sky?" Tigranes pointed at the rock, beyond which rose a thin, dirty column of faint vapor. The alarm within Gaspar sounded louder—he'd seen columns like that before.

"All halt! All halt!" Gaspar cried, reining in his horse and holding up his hand. "Tetius!"

"Yes, sir?" Tetius replied.

"Tigranes, call your fastest rider," Gaspar ordered. "Tetius, you remember when we stopped at Lur Dokis on the way in, don't you?"

"Yes, sir."

"I want you and Tigranes' man to scout out the city. Be safe, but be swift. Get close enough to observe as much as you can, but don't put yourself in danger."

"Danger, sir?"

"I don't like the look of that," Gaspar pointed to the smoke column.

"Neither do I, sir," Tetius nodded grimly. The two scouts rode off while the captains set about unpacking the weapons and arming the men. The caravan was terribly vulnerable strung out along the mountain road, but they wouldn't know whether to continue forward or turn back until the scouts reported.

Before the afternoon was half spent the two horsemen returned, riding up to Tigranes and the three lords, smelling of smoke.

"With deep sorrow, we report that the city is destroyed, my lords," Tetius said, removing his helmet.

"Destroyed?" gasped Melchior.

"Yes, my lord," replied Tigranes' scout, who was Hymeas. "The walls are broken, the city plundered, and the buildings burned. There are—none living within the walls or in the area around."

"Raiders?" asked Balthazar.

"Perhaps," Gaspar said with a knowing glance at Tigranes. Both experienced soldiers knew that it would take more than a band of mountain raiders to breach the walls of a city like Lur Dokis. "I presume from the thoroughness of your report that none of the enemy remain in the area?"

"No, sir. We spotted nobody, friend or foe," Tetius replied.

"What should we do?" Melchior asked. "Turn back?"

Gaspar pondered this. "I'm not sure. We could be just as vulnerable turning back as going forward. Also, some of our provisions are getting dangerously low."

"You won't be reprovisioning at Lur Dokis, my lord," Hymeas advised. "The enemy plundered it too thoroughly."

"I know, but there are other options," Gaspar replied. "The main question is whether it would be safe to proceed. No enemy seen, you say?"

"No, sir," Tetius replied. "Most of the ashes were cold, and there were—other signs. I'd guess a day and a half, two days since the enemy rode away."

"Here's what I suggest," Gaspar said. "Some of us should ride ahead more swiftly, while the main body follows at a slower pace. We can examine the city and surroundings more thoroughly and evaluate the risk. I think we'll be reasonably safe approaching the city. Hopefully the marauders won't be returning there soon, given that they took everything of value when they left."

So a vanguard of about twenty men rode ahead, leaving a guard to bring along the main body of the caravan. The riders thundered along the road until they turned the shoulder of rock and came into sight of the city, which was about four miles distant. Gaspar groaned in grief. The city walls were breached in a couple of places and smudged with smoke all around. The gates stood open, and all manner of debris lay about the ground before them. Gaspar's stomach turned—he knew what some of the debris would be.

Their pace slowed as they drew near the devastation, the smell of burning and death lingering heavily in the air. Clusters of vultures and kites broke up and flapped away from the intruders, hissing sullenly, while jackals growled as they slunk away from their gruesome feasts. The men looked shocked and wary, glancing around for any sign of threat. Few of them had ever seen battle or its aftermath, having spent their lives as gate guards or caravan escorts. Tetius and Gordias had seen many such scenes, and stayed close by their master, lances at the ready.

Gaspar surveyed the carnage grimly while Balthazar looked saddened and Melchior appeared shocked. There were bodies, and parts of bodies, lying all about, amidst broken household goods and smashed pottery. The bodies looked to be very young or very old, with a few badly mutilated women. Jammed into the ground near the gate were some large stakes, upon which were impaled some men of middle to old age.

"Standard retribution on city leaders for daring to defy the invaders," Gaspar explained. "You men, take them down. You others, ride a complete circuit around the area to insure all is dormant. It looks like they've moved on, but we want to be sure there are no spies lurking."

"Yes, sir," a guard replied. "And the rest of the caravan?"

"Have them camp over there," Gaspar pointed to a meadow about a mile away. "No reason to bring them closer than necessary."

The three lords, Tigranes, and a few armsmen dismounted at the gates and picked their way over the charred debris into the city. Tetius walked beside Gaspar with his gladius drawn while Gordias stayed a little ahead, arrow on string, head swiveling left and right, alert for any hint of threat. The streets were dead silent and thick with the smell of charred wood and burned flesh.

It did not take them long to survey the ruin. Lur Dokis was a typical city of its type, with but a few dozen dwellings of any size within its walls. The king's house had the distinction of being the only two-story building in the city. It had been thoroughly plundered and vandalized. The main building of the city was the temple, located in the center of town, and around it were clustered areas of common storage like the city granaries. All these were broken open and their meager contents scattered about.

"They didn't get much out of here," Tigranes observed, poking about the empty chambers. "What did they expect? It's a month until harvest—of course grain stores are going to be low."

"I don't know what they were thinking," Gaspar replied, lifting some canvas with his sword.

"Curious, sir," Gordias said. "Why didn't they fire the fields? That's what frustrated invaders usually do."

"I've been wondering about that myself," Gaspar replied. "And I've got some worrisome speculations, but let's finish inspecting this mess."

They went up into the temple, which had been stripped of anything metal and thoroughly vandalized. Some bodies lay around, particularly near the idol's throne. Balthazar guessed it was a temple to Ashurbel, though it might be to some other goddess. The temple's tiny treasury appeared to be a box tucked into a small chamber at the base of the throne. The box had been pulled out and smashed to splinters.

"Any gold the city had would have been in here," Gaspar said. "Nothing left, of course."

"I'm not sure," Balthazar said, looking about on the floor in the dark, narrow area behind the throne. He picked something up, examined it, then spent a couple of minutes on his hands and knees feeling about on the floor. He seemed to be collecting small bits of something and putting them in whatever he was holding. Eventually he turned and they could see that he'd picked up a small, ornately carved wooden casket. It looked just large enough to hold a shoe, and he had the top open.

"I suspect this was pulled out and cast aside as worthless," Balthazar said, holding out the casket so they could see the small pieces that filled it. "Which proves they're fools, if nothing else. This is probably worth more than the contents of the chest, unless it was packed to the brim with gold, which I doubt."

"What is it?" Tigranes asked.

Balthazar sniffed the box then held it out for them to do likewise. "Myrrh," he explained. "Finest dried resin. In Damascus this would be weighed out by the quarter-ounce, and I suspect there are about two pounds here."

Tigranes gave a low whistle. "How do you think the city got so much?"

"Hard to tell," Balthazar said. "Perhaps a town merchant came by some and donated it, or left it here for safekeeping. But the contents of this casket could buy at least the king's house, and probably several more."

"If I may suggest, Lord Balthazar should take custody of this treasure for the time being," Gaspar said. "I think we've seen all there is to see within the city. Let us retire to the gates and discuss our next steps."

"One thing we must do," Melchior added. "Is give these poor victims a proper burial."

At the city gates they were greeted by some of the scouts they'd sent to examine the area. A couple of them came galloping up and dismounted.

"My lords," one said. "We have surveyed the area and found no man living, friend or foe, within three miles of the city. But there is a road that leads northwest out of the valley, and we found signs that a host had passed that way recently."

Gaspar nodded grimly. "I was afraid of that. We'll discuss it later. Right now, let us tend to the fallen. We need to lay them to rest so their spirits may be at peace."

"Yes, but what can we do?" Tigranes asked. "We have neither time nor tools to dig them proper graves, and there isn't enough burnable wood left to build a pyre for so many."

"If I may suggest," Balthazar said. "Most temples have an underchamber beneath the main floor. If this one does, and it proves suitable, we could use it as a crypt for the fallen."

This suggestion was accepted. The temple did have a small underchamber, and the rest of the day was spent locating all the bodies and transporting them there. The chamber entrances were sealed and Balthazar, who knew some of the rites of Ashurbel, committed them to death. Then they retired to their camp to discuss what to do next. Though nobody had much appetite, Gaspar encouraged them all to eat and rest as they could, and set Tigranes to drawing up a watch schedule. Tonight everyone would sleep with weapons near.

As the sun dropped toward the west, Gaspar met with Tigranes and the two other lords.

"Based on what we've seen, I'm guessing that we're not dealing with a small group of mountain bandits," Gaspar explained. "I think this is the work of an organized band of marauders, like a small army."

"Right here in the heart of the empire?" Melchior asked. "Ctesiphon is only a few days' ride from here. Ecbatana is just over those mountains. How would they dare?"

"The valleys in this region run from northwest to southeast. Marauders can pass up and down them without coming near a royal road," cautioned Gaspar. "Ecbatana is further than it seems. It may be close as the crow flies, but it is further by land travel, which requires crossing many mountains and valleys. When we did that escort job to Ctesiphon a few months ago, I heard a rumor of raiders from Hyrcania sweeping into the area. Perhaps this was the work of such a group."

"What should we do?" Tigranes asked.

Gaspar tapped his sword hilt and pursed his lips in thought. "Had I a couple centuries of legionaries, I would hunt them down and crush them. But by ourselves, we are no match for any serious armed force. We should try to get ourselves to safety, and notify the Empire of this incursion as quickly as we may."

"Should we turn around? Head back the way we came?" asked Melchior.

"That is an option," Gaspar acknowledged. "But we don't know exactly which way the enemy has gone. Any direction we travel may be toward danger. Also, we took a day and a half to get here; retracing our route would take at least two more. Once back on the main road, it would be another three or four days to Ctesiphon, which would be the closest place we'd find any Imperial officials to notify. That's nearly a week of travel, by which time our information would be too old to be of any use. The marauders could be almost anywhere by then."

"Also, our provisions are running thin," Tigranes pointed out.

"Is there an alternative?" Balthazar asked.

"There is, but I'm reluctant to suggest it," Gaspar explained. "The chief road through this valley goes over a low pass at the northwest end and down into the next valley. There is a city named Alwenah, similar to Lur Dokis but a bit smaller. The two cities had the varied relationship you'd expect: usually rivals, sometimes enemies, occasionally allies, often trading partners.

Since my main contacts were in Lur Dokis, I don't know much about Alwenah other than they're there. If they'd let us pass through their valley, that would get us back to the main road in maybe three days, just past Ctesiphon, where we could send riders back to alert the Imperial officials. But going that way would require the good will of Alwenah, and there may be another danger."

"What would that be?" asked Melchior.

"There's a possibility the marauders which destroyed Lur Dokis moved on to that valley. Though there's an equal possibility they arrived from that direction, which may mean that Alwenah has suffered the same fate as Lur Dokis. There's no way to know without looking."

"Could we send scouts?" Tigranes asked.

"I seem to remember that Alwenah is tucked away on the northeast side of the valley, and that the valley floor has many hummocks. You can't see the city easily from the valley road, which means riding across the hills and dales until you can. Even if we dispatched swift scouts first thing in the morning, it would take them half a day to get within sight of the city, observe, and return—and that's presuming safe riding. I'm loath to take that much time."

"What do you recommend?" Melchior asked.

Gaspar thought for a minute, glancing at Tigranes as if for support. "I think we need to move, all of us, and soon. We don't want to linger in this valley—the marauders may come back this way. Getting back to the main road as quickly as possible is important, as is getting the most current information to the officials in Ctesiphon. Those considerations all indicate moving forward through the next valley. As I mentioned, the valley road is fairly distant from the city, so we may be able to pass through without anyone noticing."

"Might we be able to reprovision?" Balthazar asked.

"It's…possible," Gaspar said, glancing again at Tigranes. "We'll evaluate that once we get there." Both of the military men seemed to think that just making it through the valley and back to the relative safety of the main road would be achievement enough.

"Very well," Melchior concluded. "Captain Tigranes, pass the word that we will be breaking camp first thing in the morning and proceeding into the next valley."

"Yes, sir," Tigranes said, and they all broke up to return to their own pavilions. Gaspar sought out Tigranes as he returned to his duties.

"Captain?"

"Yes, my lord?"

"Set an extra guard tonight, and insure all campfires are smothered. Tell the men to be prepared for anything tomorrow."

"Yes, sir," Tigranes replied. Though he was officially in charge of the caravan's security, he was not about to ignore advice from an experienced field commander like Gaspar.

The tension was thick as the caravan broke camp in the gray pre-dawn. The uncertainty and hint of danger made everyone edgy, and nobody wanted to linger in the doomed valley. But even the swiftest hands take a while to pack up a camp of that size, and the sun was well above the horizon before the column moved out. Tigranes had spread the guards along the length of the caravan as best he could, but the thin line of lances only served to remind him of how little protection they actually had.

They moved as quickly as they could along the valley road and up the gentle slope to the pass. The rise between the valleys was barely more than a line of hills. As the caravan descended the far side, they could see the valley floor was thick with hummocks and hollows, mottled by fields that were approaching ripeness. As Gaspar had said, Alwenah was not visible from the valley road. Gaspar scanned the sky for any smoky columns or brown smudging. He saw none, but neither did he see any people scattered about the hills or working the fields.

The caravan descended to where another road split off from the valley road, heading northward along the face of the hills that formed the southeast wall of the valley.

"This road leads toward Alwenah," Gaspar explained. "I, at least, would like to ride it far enough to see how the city fares. If possible, Lord Melchior, I would like to take Captain Tigranes with me, and perhaps a few guards.

Melchior and Balthazar looked at each other. They clearly thought a swift, quiet passage through the valley was what the situation called for, but they recognized the need for good information, and were reluctant to gainsay their experienced military member.

"We will come, too," Melchior said.

"Very well," Gaspar replied. "You four, come with us." He waved some guards to their side. "You others, keep everyone moving, but slowly. Keep watch, and if you suspect any threats, stop and circle. We shouldn't be long."

The small group rode swiftly up the road toward the city. The hills to their right steepened quickly, becoming craggy and harsh. About half a mile up the road Gaspar spotted a trail that ran up the face of the hills. "We should get a good view from up there," he pointed, steering his horse up the trail. They soon reached a level spot, partly shielded by boulders. "Ride slower, everyone—we don't want to raise a lot of dust. Men, lower your lances." They looked out over the variegated terrain toward the city and gasped.

The small city of Alwenah lay near the northern edge of the valley, almost up against the mountains that formed the far wall. They could see that the city gates were closed, and around the walls lay a dirty, sprawling mob. There were horses and tents and smoking fires and refuse pits. There was some kind of activity near the gates, but otherwise the scene was quiet with the discordant edge that indicated a lull in the battle rather than true peace.

"So now we know," Gaspar said in a flat voice. "Where the army that raped Lur Dokis went."

The three lords stared in horror while the guards fidgeted nervously. The city lay no more than four miles away, and a sharp-eyed enemy could spot them where they stood if he looked in the right place.

Gaspar ground his teeth and looked at his companions, who were gazing, stunned, at the scene before them. The memory of what they'd seen at Lur Dokis was still fresh in their minds—the shattered walls, the burned timbers, the bodies scattered about, and the stench of death. Now the people of Alwenah seemed doomed to the same end.

"Bastards," Gaspar muttered, gripping his saddle. Melchior paled and hung his head in grief.

"Maybe…" Balthazar offered weakly. "It is their *kismet*, their fate."

"The wickedness of the world," moaned Melchior. "What can be done?"

Gaspar wheeled in the saddle, his blood rising, and stared at his colleagues. "Fate? The world's wickedness? My lords, you surprise and disappoint me! That," he pointed at the besieging army, "Is no random turn of fortune! That is not the frown of the gods! That is wicked men stealing and killing because they can steal and kill! That is lawlessness, plain and simple! Faugh! If only we could get word to Ctesiphon in time!" He slammed his hand on his saddle in frustration. "If only I had three centuries of men—or even two!—I would stop this barbarism here and now!"

"You think…against that many?" Balthazar asked, staring at the army.

"Bah!" scoffed Gaspar. "Many of those are camp followers or slaves—probably some captured at Lur Dokis. I'd wager that the count of the fighting men is no more than a cohort— between four and five hundred. All mounted, of course, and dangerous archers, but there are ways of dealing with that. Ah! If I only had the men!" He glared across the valley, muttering under his breath.

Tigranes edged his horse forward until he was just behind the three magi. Pointing toward the city, he said in a voice just loud enough for them to hear:

"My lords, do not turn and look, but there are archers moving into position among the rocks up the hill to our right."

The men sat rigid and tried not to turn toward the threat. The air grew so still that they thought they could hear some of the clamor from the army around the city.

"Any behind us, Tigranes?" asked Gaspar.

"I don't know, sir, but I assume so. I don't want to turn and look."

Balthazar and Melchior were whitening and their hands trembled. Gaspar drew a deep breath, his mind racing. They were in no position to fight off an ambush, and could not outrun arrows. Glancing again at the army surrounding the city, he whispered to his companions, "Trust me." Backing his horse and turning to face the hill, he rose in his saddle and called out in loud, clear Greek.

"We are travelers transiting the valley! We are not part of that barbarian army! We only wish to pass in peace, and help as we may!"

There was a minute's silence before about a dozen archers rose from their cover, bows drawn and arrows pointed right at the travelers. Nobody moved, but Gaspar noticed that the archer's garb did not look like barbarian gear.

One of the archers began working his way down through the boulders, keeping his arrow trained on them. When he got within hailing distance, he called out,

"Who are you? Whence do you come?"

"I am called Gaspar. This is Balthazar. We are outlanders, but our master Melchior is of Parthia. He lives near Seleucia, which is where we began our journey."

"Seleucia? On Tigris?" the man asked.

"On Eulaeus—several weeks' journey," Gaspar answered. "These others are our guards, who will not draw weapons against you." He nodded to the guards, who reluctantly dropped their lances on the ground and put their hands on their saddle bows.

The man who had spoken lowered his bow and came closer. He looked dirty and weary. "I must take you to my captain, Datis," he announced.

"Then you are not of the marauders?" Gaspar asked for confirmation.

"No," the man replied. "I am Kigdagatas. I am of Alwenah, as are my men—what few of us there are."

"We have just come from Lur Dokis," Gaspar said. "We grieve for your troubles. How comes it that you are not within the city?"

"My captain must answer that. Come with me. Your guards may bring their lances."

They were led along the trail to a hollow in a gully that was clearly the home to many ill-equipped men. There were only a handful of horses, and blankets or shawls were draped across bushes or between rocks as makeshift tents. They were brought to a large flat rock that was waist height, where stood a few men who were the only ones wearing armor. One wore a plumed helmet. They looked like the ranking officers of a small city's guard or militia, and their gear had seen many years. The least of Melchior's guards was better equipped.

The travelers were brought before the man in the plumed helmet. They dismounted and bowed to him.

"I am Gaspar. This is Lord Balthazar, the Lord Melchior, and Tigranes, the captain of our guard. We are chance travelers through your valley. We mean no harm to the people of your city."

"I wish that could be said of all who have come here," the man replied. "I am Datis, captain of the army of Alwenah—for all that means." He looked haggard and worn, as did the men behind him.

Gaspar nodded grimly. "We have just come from Lur Dokis, where I had friends—Arazis, Teispes the horse trader, and Salabus the blacksmith. We grieve their loss."

"None of those are names I know, but we, too, grieve at the fall of our neighbors," Datis replied. "We caught wind of marauders in that valley. After all traffic through the pass ceased, my king sent me and some men by shepherd's paths to spy out what was happening. We arrived too late—when we came down from the hills, the city had been sacked and burned. The ashes were still warm. Fearing where the marauders may have gone next, we went hot-foot back to our valley to find our worst fears realized: our city besieged, and our loved ones inside."

"How many are you?" Gaspar asked.

"Our party numbered six dozen or so when we set out," Datis explained. "But only four dozen are properly armed. We have gathered shepherds and hillmen from our valley and around Lur Dokis. We now number nearly ten dozen."

"Too few for a direct assault," Gaspar murmured. "How is your supply situation?"

"Regarding arms, moderate. Almost all have bows, some have swords, a handful have long weapons. We have ten horses among us. The hillmen have no metal weapons but swear by their slings."

"You have slingers?" Gaspar asked with interest, starting to pace as he thought. "That's good. How are your victuals?"

"Poor. We only went out equipped for a journey of two days at most. That was three nights ago now—we're out of food."

"The marauders—do they patrol the valley? Guard the passes or roads?"

"Not that we can tell," Datis answered. "They stay close to the city, shooting over the walls and battering the gate at times."

"Aye, aye," Gaspar muttered, pacing and stroking his beard. "And we have three dozen or so, well-armed and trained...ah, if only we had a map of the valley."

"But we do," Datis said, gesturing one of his men forward. "The king wanted to be sure we marked the enemy's position and movement, so he sent us with maps of our valley and that of Lur Dokis." The aide drew some scrolls from a pouch. "They are simply drawn, but accurate."

"Do you have men who know the details of the local terrain?" Gaspar asked.

"The hillmen know it like their own skin," Datis said as he unrolled the scroll on the rock.

"We can do this deed!" Gaspar said fiercely. "Captain, we have about three dozen men-at-arms, all mounted. If we combine forces, I can come up with a plan to defeat the marauders."

"Against so many?" Datis asked. "What hope do we have?"

"We have surprise. We have the advantage of position," Gaspar said, tapping the map. "We know the area, they do not. All we have to do is come up with a plan that strips them of their advantage while maximizing ours. With this map and the advice of your hillmen, I think I can draw up such a plan."

"How soon?" Datis asked.

"Hopefully by tomorrow morning," Gaspar said. "Don't look so surprised, Captain! I've fought all over the Roman empire. This kind of planning is my specialty. Can you bring me some hillmen?"

"Yes, sir," Datis beckoned to one of the other men, who dashed away.

Gaspar turned to Balthazar and Melchior. "We must do this. We can't just leave them."

The magi looked at each other. "You're right," said Balthazar. "We can't."

"Well said. Tigranes, could I have your help?" Gaspar asked, bending over the map and considering the forces at his disposal. This would be a challenge of a type he'd never faced before. His mind raced and churned, swirling around one central question.

What would Alexander do?

ENGAGEMENT

Baba sat tensely in the saddle, trying to keep his camel still, watching the ridge to the east. It was growing lighter there, but that wasn't enough—they had to see the edge of the rising sun top the mountains. Those were their instructions. Fortunately, he wasn't the one who had to make the call as to when the sun had cleared the horizon. He was just helping Lord Balthazar, who was seated on the fifth camel over and watching the ridge as well. He looked a little tense, too, which seemed odd, seeing as how he was not only a grownup, but a lord. But on this trip Baba was learning that grownups could be afraid, and get nervous about doing things properly, just like youngsters could.

And he didn't even have a hard job. All he had to do was herd the camels.

Nobody had gotten much sleep the night before. Lord Gaspar had been like a madman, hammering people with questions, barking orders, rethinking plans, and pacing, always pacing. Men had run to and fro and riders had dashed about. Fortunately, the sky was clear and the moon was just past full, so there was enough light for people to travel by. The strange men from the valley had joined the caravan and eaten them out of the rest of their supplies. The cook and steward had been a little put out by this, until Captain Tigranes had quietly explained that if this action succeeded they could reprovision at the city, and if it failed it wouldn't matter anyway. This had sobered them both, and Baba as well.

Baba wasn't clear on all the details of the plan. He knew that a couple of hours ago a larger group of men had gone southwest, while a smaller band of men had gone due west, all guided by the scruffy-looking hillmen. Lord Gaspar, Captain Tigranes, the camels, and most of the horsemen had ridden to a spot along the eastern edge of the valley, well north of the valley road. They'd herded the camels into this little hollow along the valley wall, where the last task of the long night had been chopping bushes and tying ropes and trying to keep the camels calm and in order. Baba was proud to have been selected for this mission, not least because of his proven aptitude with the camels. Lord Balthazar was one of the few who had experience riding the beasts, and he and Baba were the only men who could be spared from the fighting forces.

Now it came down to this, watching and waiting for the sunrise. Hopefully all the men were in their places and remembering their instructions. The camels, snorting and jostling one another, were skittish about their unusual restraints and anxious to be moving. Baba whistled and called to them, urging them to stay in position and not get the ropes all tangled. The eastern sky beyond the mountains was growing lighter and lighter.

"Ready, Baba?" called Lord Balthazar.

"Yes, my lord!" Baba replied.

"And…there it is! Go, Baba!" Lord Balthazar cried. "Yah! Yah!"

With shouts and calls the two men charged out of the hollow, the herd of camels following behind. The beasts instinctively spread out to make room, and were somewhat startled at what they found dragging behind them, but they were accustomed to unusual loads. With cries and slaps of the quirts, the two urged their own camels to a run and steered them toward the ridge that had been pointed out. The rest of the herd galloped along behind, setting a good pace across the dusty, scrub-strewn valley floor.

"There they go!" Tigranes called unnecessarily. The charge of the camels, which was the trigger event for the entire venture, was plainly visible from the low ridge on which they stood. Soon the dust cloud being thrown up would be visible across the entire valley—which was the whole point.

Gaspar watched from where he stood paused in his pacing. Being mounted would give him a better vantage point from which to observe, but he was too nervous and his horse was picking up on that. It all came down to this. The planning, the briefings, the hurried troop placements in the night—all to set the stage for right now. The next hour would decide it all. At the end of it, they'd either be victorious or dead.

"They're spreading out nicely," Tigranes observed. "Baba knows what he's doing." One of their worries had been that the camels would bunch together and entangle themselves in their ropes. But the camels were spreading out sufficiently not to endanger one another, and the shrubs and branches they were dragging were raising a cloud of dust.

"I was never worried about Baba," Gaspar said. "Balthazar gave me some concern. He admitted that it's been decades since he's ridden a camel, and he's never raced one."

"They both seem to be doing fine," Tigranes replied. "Look at them go."

"Camels are ideal for this task," Gaspar acknowledged. "They can gallop over rough terrain that would slow a horse, and they can drag those branches without problem."

"Do you think the enemy will notice the dust?"

"Against the sunrise? It'll be impossible to miss. You've got Hymeas stationed up there keeping an eye on the city?" Gaspar pointed to the top of the hillock behind which they were sheltered.

"Yes, sir. He has orders to report any activity," Tigranes answered.

"I'm guessing that it won't be long," Gaspar said, watching the dust cloud rise against the morning sunlight as the camels galloped across the valley.

The greatest worry of any besieging army was relief forces arriving to challenge them. This was doubly true of an army of mounted marauders who did their fighting on horseback and dared not be caught on foot, where they were ill-equipped to fight. Gaspar guessed that this marauder band, wherever they'd come from, would be especially wary of the arrival of Imperial troops, since these valleys weren't all that far from the main road and population centers like Ctesiphon. The marauders' lookouts would be constantly watching for any signs of an approaching enemy. Signs like a large cloud of dust rising from the direction of the pass—a cloud of dust that might be raised by columns of cavalry riding into the valley.

"My lord! Captain!" Hymeas came scrambling down from his vantage point to report. "Activity in the enemy camp! They seem to be mounting and forming up!"

"So far, so good," Gaspar nodded grimly. "The next step is up to our brave 'scouts'."

Baba and Balthazar slowed as they approached the ridge. Baba's keen eyes spotted the small stream that the hillmen had told them they'd find there. They steered the camels toward it, and once the beasts had slowed to a walk, Baba leapt down and dashed about with his knife, cutting the ropes to free the camels of their burdens. They didn't need to be driven to the water, but found it readily enough as Baba and Balthazar tugged and kicked the brush out of the path.

"Well, lad," Balthazar asked, looking at the long cloud of red dust hanging in the morning air. "Think we've done our part?"

"I...I hope so, my lord," Baba replied, still a little abashed to be speaking so casually with one of the lords.

"Well, let's get up there to see how things unfold," Balthazar pointed up the ridge to the vantage point they were supposed to reach. Baba scrambled quickly up the rocky slope, followed more slowly by the older man. Looking back and seeing Balthazar's slower pace, Baba hesitated.

"Get on, lad, get on," the Arab waved to him. "I'll catch up." So Baba proceeded to the flat outcropping that enabled them to look out over most of the valley. The variations in the valley floor hid the base of the city—all they could see was the top of the wall and the buildings. This meant they couldn't see the enemy army clustered around the wall. But if Lord Gaspar's plans worked out, that wouldn't matter, because much of the enemy would soon be coming to them.

Or at least near enough, Baba thought nervously, glancing toward the rocky gully that lay just to the west of the ridge.

"See anything yet, lad?" Lord Balthazar asked as he climbed panting onto the ledge.

"Oh—ah, not yet, my lord," Baba replied, suddenly remembering his lookout responsibilities. He scanned the hills toward the middle of the valley, looking for the two horsemen that Lord Gaspar had sent there. At first he saw nothing but scrub-covered mounds between fields of grain. But then he spotted movement, a couple of miles away, on the south side of a low ridge that was close to the city.

"There—there they are, my lord!" Baba called, pointing. Two horsemen were just riding up to the top of the ridge.

Lord Gaspar had explained that those two horsemen would have the most dangerous job of any that fateful morning. They had three tasks: to appear to be scouts of the type that would be sent out by an approaching force, to allow themselves to be spotted by the enemy, and to ride like mad with an army at their heels. They would be pulling death's beard. A chance arrow, an unlucky stone under a hoof, or even a much faster enemy rider could mean swift and savage death for either or both. Nor would the end of their mad career be any too safe. Nevertheless, many had volunteered, and Captain Tigranes had chosen two—one from the valley folk and one from their own guard, both young and wiry, both brave and skilled on horseback. They were given the swiftest, most high-spirited steeds and sent out in the cold pre-dawn to taunt a dangerous foe into a deadly chase.

Now Baba could see the two riders reach the top of the distant ridge to stand silhouetted against the morning sky in plain view. He bit his lip as the men held their position, watching the enemy; bait to draw them into a lethal trap.

"Where are they, lad? My old eyes—", Balthazar was scanning the valley floor in vain.

"There, my lord. Just atop that hill—see them?"

"Yes, yes, thank you," Balthazar said, then scowled. "I also see that." He pointed beyond the hill to the dust cloud starting to rise from the direction of the city. The enemy was coming.

The most delicate and dangerous part of the task of the two 'scouts' was to lead the enemy force at just the right distance. Not so close as to get caught, obviously, but not so far that the enemy would have a chance to observe and think about where they were being led. Gaspar's strategy for this part of the evolution hinged on the hope that the enemy was a bunch of hard-riding hotheads without a tactical thinker among them—or at least they had to act like that for the duration of the chase across the valley. The two horsemen had to maintain the appearance of a couple of frightened scouts who had stumbled across the enemy force and were now fleeing back toward their army to warn them. Hopefully this would goad the enemy into the hottest possible pursuit, in hopes of catching the "army" unaware.

The dust cloud in the direction of the city was growing, but still the two horsemen watched from the top of their hill. Baba was getting nervous—the hill on which they stood was barely a mile from the city, which meant the enemy had to be approaching, maybe even within bowshot range. There! The two 'scouts' wheeled and galloped down the ridge. Baba held his breath—it was wonderful and terrible at the same time to watch the horsemen's wild career across the valley floor. They rode like madmen, light in the saddle, weaving with dazzling skill as they guided their mounts around obstacles. The horses' feet flew so swiftly that Baba could see only a blur. His heart rose in excitement.

Then the force chasing them poured over the hilltop, and Baba gasped in terror. Lord Gaspar had guessed that perhaps twelve score of the enemy could be lured away from the city, fifteen score if they were lucky. Baba had not envisioned how many warriors that would be. He saw now, and the sight staggered him. A seemingly endless wave of howling horsemen galloped into sight, hot on the heels of the two riders.

"They...cut it rather close," Balthazar muttered in an unsteady voice. Baba was glad he had held his tongue—he didn't trust himself to keep his voice steady. The riders were barely two furlongs ahead of the enemy, and though they were riding like nothing Baba had ever seen, it still might not be enough. The enemy was riding hard, too, mounted on the swift and sturdy ponies that could go all day and still charge fiercely at the end. The enemy warriors wore the furs and leather jerkins that were common among the mountain barbarians. Baba could not see their faces but he could hear their wicked cries and see the occasional flash of a naked blade. Every so often an arrow arced through the air, but the two horsemen kept enough weave in their galloping that they made difficult targets. Baba watched exhilarated, riveted, and terrified as the deadly race pounded across the rises and hollows of the valley floor, heading for the gully.

The gully was their first and greatest hope. It cut into the southwest valley wall, almost large enough to be a small valley of its own, with a wide mouth and flattened sides and a broad, clear floor. But the sides steepened as the gully cut deeper into the valley wall, growing rockier until toward the end they were nearly cliffs. The gully floor was strewn with rocks and jutting stones that made riding impossible. The gully ended in a rough cliff face, but that could only be seen once you rounded a steep shoulder of rock that stood only a quarter mile from the end.

Hopefully the enemy would not spot that until it was too late.

All night long archers and slingers had been moving into position around the gully. With their bare hands, daggers, and stray branches they had dug and pried and pushed to destabilize boulders at strategic location until they could be set rolling with minimal effort. They'd sought out covered vantage points from which to fire. Now they waited in hiding for the enemy—who outnumbered them at least three to one—to come to them.

Slowly the sound of distant cries could be heard piercing the still morning air. Soon followed the steady, ominous thunder of hundreds of hooves riding hard. The enemy force was still chasing the two horsemen, blood in their eyes, neither observing nor considering where they were being led.

The archers and slingers ringing the gully crouched low behind their cover, quiet and unseen. A watcher stationed by the gully mouth, standing in a spot that was only visible further down the gully, turned and waved thrice. Another watcher who was sheltered halfway back in the gully relayed the signal on. The enemy was within half a mile of the gully mouth—if they were going to turn aside, they'd have to do it soon.

They didn't turn aside. Neither stopping nor slowing, they hurtled headlong after their quarry, probably thinking—if they were thinking at all—that the two horsemen would lead them to the army whose dust they'd seen against the sunrise.

With cries and a swift clatter of hooves the two horsemen charged into the gully mouth. This last stretch was among the most dangerous they'd ridden—the gully floor was smooth, but still had occasional rocks strewn about. A stumble here would mean a swift and bloody death under enemy blades. But at the far end of the gully two long ropes dangled down the cliff face, with teams of men standing ready to haul them up swiftly.

All the horsemen had to do was reach the ropes.

The horsemen were well down the gully, necessarily slowed by the need to ride more carefully, when their pursuit closed to about a furlong. Arrows began flying, but then the two horsemen turned behind the shoulder of rock and passed out of range again. Galloping madly with the last of their horses' strength, they reached the cliff and leapt from their saddles, grasping the waiting ropes. The teams started hauling them up, but they were still in terrible danger, dangling exposed to every enemy archer for a perilous length of time—and there was always the possibility that an arrow might sever a rope.

The enemy came pouring around the bend. Seeing their quarry halfway up the cliff face, they unleashed a flurry of arrows, most of which struck the rock harmlessly. The horsemen curled up behind the only protection they had—thick leather back plates, helmets, and neck guards, all designed to stop most arrows. They cried out as the arrows struck them, for even those that bounced off felt like sharp blows. One of the horsemen screamed as an arrow struck his forearm, which fell limp. But he clung the harder with his good arm, and was pulled to safety with his companion. By that time the marauders' fury had abated enough for them to look about and assess where they found themselves.

But it was too late.

As soon as the last of the enemy horsemen had swept into the gully, a watcher waved a signal, and teams of men pried on branches to loosen boulders and stacked piles of rocks. Even as the marauders were reining in to loose arrows at the taunters who had led them on the merry chase, a small avalanche cascaded down the slopes near the gully mouth, strewing the floor with rocky debris. The debris didn't block the passage, but it didn't have to. All it had to do was litter the ground enough to make the way impassable for a horse and rider.

Suddenly finding themselves in very unsuitable terrain, with the two horsemen being lifted to safety and ominous sounds to their rear, the marauders began to realize that things were not as they might appear. Wheeling and shouting, several of them tried to gain control of the situation. But just then the archers and slingers that ringed the gully began their bombardment.

"Yes!" cried Baba as the rain of death began pouring down on the trapped horsemen. From their vantage point they could see most of the gully floor, including straight down the last quarter mile, beyond the rock shoulder, where most of the enemy was concentrated. The boy danced and cheered at the enemy's discomfiture. Balthazar, who had seen battles close up, watched in grim silence. Gaspar's audacious plan seemed to be working so far. But much more had to work as planned if the enemy was to be defeated.

Surrounding the gully, the valley defenders had all the advantages and pressed them mercilessly. Shooting from sheltered positions on high ground, their initial volleys devastated the enemy force. The marauders returned fire, but many foolishly tried to stay on their horses, which was their most familiar battle posture. But in the wheeling confusion even their deadly archery availed little against the well-hidden defenders, and those who tried to fight from horseback quickly died there.

The marauders who survived longer did so by dismounting and attempting to fight on foot, but even that proved difficult. To reach their enemy they had to climb uphill across rocky terrain in the face of lethal fire from well-sheltered defenders.

There were rocks and ridges to hide behind, but that didn't do the marauders any good. As far as the defenders were concerned, a pinned enemy was as good as a dead one, at least temporarily, since it enabled them to turn their fire to more active targets. The defending archers had to choose their marks carefully and shoot true, making the most of their arrow supply, but the slingers were proving their worth several times over. The rocky terrain provided them an inexhaustible source of ammunition, their aim was deadly, and the relatively short range meant their projectiles struck with brutal force. The gully floor was soon strewn with the maimed, stunned, and dead, while horses and men darted and wheeled in confusion, looking for any way out of the deadly trap.

Eventually a large, imposing warrior began to grab his fellow marauders, yelling at them in their outlandish tongue. He clearly realized that so long as they were scattered and unfocused, they were nothing but targets. Slapping and shoving his panicking comrades into a semblance of a formation, he got several of them to start moving up the west wall of the gully. Their small, round shields were better suited for mounted battle, but they were better than nothing. Crouching low and holding their shields high, a wedge of the marauders began slowly working its way over the rocky terrain toward their tormentors.

"I don't like the look of that," Balthazar said, pointing to the small formation advancing up the slope. The valley defenders were spread in a loose ring around the edge of the gully and had few hand weapons—short swords, a few shields, and no lances or spears. One of the weaknesses of the deployment was that any breakout from the gully could quickly destroy or scatter a sizeable number of the thinly spread defenders—and a breakout looked to be just what was about to happen.

"Lad, how fast can you ride one of those camels?" Balthazar asked.

"Fast enough," Baba replied.

"Get back to Gaspar and get help. A dozen mounted warriors should be enough, but they need to get here quickly!"

"Yes, my lord!" gasped Baba as he clambered down the ridge. Grabbing the halter of his favorite camel, a large bull he'd named Xerxes, Baba hoisted himself into the saddle and turned the beast's head toward where the other force stood waiting for their time.

Xerxes made good speed straight across the valley floor. It was only about four miles to where Lord Gaspar and Captain Tigranes waited, and Baba slapped Xerxes with the quirt as he peered toward his goal anxiously. Then he noticed something moving off to his left. Looking carefully, he saw that it was a horseman. So soon? And alone? They weren't supposed to move just—

With a gasp Baba realized that the lone horsemen was one of the enemy. What he was doing riding solo across the valley, Baba did not know, but the horseman had spotted Baba and was riding hard to intercept him.

"Come on, Xerxes," Baba urged, his heart pounding. He was unarmed, having only his belt knife, and was no match for a full-grown, fully armed barbarian warrior. Evasion was impossible—even now the rider was closing on Baba's course, a quarter mile dead ahead, and turning to come straight at him. The rider's bow was out and Baba almost screamed as an arrow came flying toward him. It fell well short, but he still ducked and stayed low, breathing heavily. He'd never had anyone target him with a lethal weapon, and he didn't like it one bit. His throat was tight and his bladder wanted to empty. Another arrow flew nearer, and he slid sideways in the saddle, plastering himself as best he could against the side of Xerxes' thick neck. Yet another arrow whizzed past, and Baba wondered if the man would shoot Xerxes. Then he realized that the rider would hardly risk damaging such a valuable piece of plunder as the camel. No, it was Baba the man was trying to kill, as quickly and efficiently as possible.

Petrified, Baba peered under Xerxes' neck at the swiftly closing rider, who was now but two furlongs distant. The rider had drawn his sword and was coming straight at them. Baba guessed that he intended to take a cut as he rode by, and then circle around behind Xerxes and come up the other side, where Baba would be an easy target for the rider's arrows. What could he do? Baba had only seconds to decide.

What the enemy doesn't expect. He'd been hearing Lord Gaspar say that all night—what doesn't the enemy expect? That's what we need to do.

What didn't this rider expect Baba to do?

Abruptly Baba sat up in the saddle and yanked Xerxes' left rein, causing him to veer into the path of the oncoming horse. Startled by the vast bulk of the camel abruptly changing course, the horse shied slightly. The rider, who was rising in his saddle loops and raising his sword to slice at Baba's unprotected leg, was startled by both the camel's swerve and Baba's sudden reappearance. Lowering his sword to clutch at his reins, the rider was distracted just at the moment that the horse and camel passed each other.

Instinctively Baba lashed out with the only weapon he had— the stiff leather quirt in his left hand. Catching the rider across his torso and knocking the sword from his hand, the quirt's force was amplified by the combined momentum of the two galloping beasts. Baba's arm felt nearly yanked from its socket, but the rider fared even worse. Already unstable in his half-standing position, and trying to hold his bow and sword and reins all at once, he was knocked backwards out of his saddle. Clutching desperately, he toppled over the rear of his horse and was caught with one foot entangled in his saddle loops. He fell screaming to the ground as his pony ran faster, frightened by the commotion. Baba looked over his shoulder to see the man writhing and screaming as he was dragged over the rough ground, his horse galloping in terror.

Baba exhaled. There. He had faced death and vanquished his first enemy. But instead of feeling triumphant and exhilarated, he felt nauseated and light-headed. He wanted nothing so much as to stop Xerxes, vomit behind a rock, and empty his bladder and bowels. But he had no time. The whole terrifying incident had transpired in less time than it took to run a mile. Xerxes kept galloping as if nothing unusual had just happened. The rise where Lord Gaspar's force lay hidden was about two miles away. He couldn't stop for anything, no matter what he wanted to do, because his message needed to get through or relief might not arrive on time. He swallowed hard and kept riding, trying to slow his breathing.

Concerned faces met Baba when he rode up to where the warriors were waiting. They'd been able to watch his gallop across the valley, and certainly his close brush with the rider.

"Lad, are you all right?" Captain Tigranes asked as he helped Baba down.

"All right—thirsty—arm hurts," Baba gasped, then stood up. "Captain—the gully—need reinforcements."

Captain Tigranes and Lord Gaspar looked at each other, as if hearing something they'd expected. "Go," said Gaspar with a jerk of his head, and Tigranes swung back into the saddle. Nearby stood about a score of mounted guards with lances— clearly they'd anticipated Baba's message. "Be back as quickly as you may—time is short." The horses thundered off while Baba crouched on the ground. Lord Gaspar himself pushed a waterskin into his hands, but he managed only a swallow before vomiting into the dirt.

"That was bravely ridden," Lord Gaspar said at his shoulder. "I'm proud of you."

"It...it was terrible," Baba gasped.

"It's always terrible, lad," Gaspar said quietly.

"That poor man," Baba said, not caring what anyone might think.

"Indeed," Lord Gaspar echoed. "We can only hope he was knocked unconscious quickly. There's a latrine behind those bushes, if you need."

Back at the gully, the situation for the defenders was getting desperate. Rallying behind the large, grim warrior, the wedge of marauders was steadily working its way up the western slope. Some defenders were running to help the handful that were trying to hold back the advance, but that left other areas around the gully perimeter undefended. The archers were running low on arrows, and though the slingers were felling a few, enough of the marauders were still advancing.

As the enemy approached within fifty yards of the edge, most of the defenders started scattering before the threat. Two brave archers remained. As the leader of the marauders looked up the slope with fiery eyes and set teeth, the archers let fly their last arrows, cast aside their bows, and drew their short swords. One of the arrows found its mark in the neck of a marauder, but the other was swatted aside by the leader's shield. With a roar the foe charged up the final yards and clear of the gully. The two archers were brutally cut down, and the marauders poured over the edge, looking for defenders to attack.

Even as the defenders were scattering, stopping long enough to fire one last arrow or rock before fleeing, the thunder of hooves echoed from the rocks. Up the broad west edge along the top of the gully rode Tigranes' squadron, lances lowered, shields up. The defenders scattered from their path and the marauders found themselves in the worst position infantry could be: facing a cavalry charge with no spears or projectile weapons. The leader stood bravely, facing the horses with his naked sword, but Tigranes himself ran the marauder down, pinning him to the ground. Then all was mayhem as the cavalry rode through the foe again and again, slashing and trampling. Then the cavalry drew back, leaving the savaged enemy infantry ringed by archers. Now the marauders were truly trapped—to stay where they were meant slow death by arrows, but to charge the archers would trigger another cavalry assault.

"Wait!" Tigranes called to the archers. Turning to the knot of marauders, he cried out in Greek and again in Aramaic: "Do you cry quarter?"

A heavily accented voice called back in Aramaic: "Quarter! Quarter!"

"Quarter is granted," Tigranes cried. "Drop your weapons and come kneel here."

The cry was taken up around the rim of the gully. "Quarter is granted! Quarter is granted!" The enemy who'd reached the gully edge came and knelt in a line where Tigranes indicated. One warrior with a bad scalp cut spoke Aramaic, and Tigranes had him translate into the marauders' barbarian tongue.

"My men will bind you, but you will not be killed. Your wounded will be treated as best we can. If you break quarter, you will all be slaughtered."

"Can you help us round them up?" asked one of the archers as Tigranes walked over to retrieve his lance.

"We cannot—we must get back," Tigranes replied, looking down at where the great enemy warrior lay with the lance through his chest. "This one was a brave fighter."

"He cost many lives," the archer replied.

"Nonetheless," Tigranes answered, pulling his lance free. "Offer them the chance to tend their wounded and bury their fallen."

"Yes, sir."

VICTORY

Gaspar breathed a sigh of relief as he saw Tigranes bring the squadron galloping back. The enemy was already sending solo scouts riding around the valley. Gaspar had to act before any word got back to the enemy's camp of the fate of the first force they'd sent out.

"Losses?" Gaspar asked as Tigranes rode up.

"One horse lamed—we left him back—and another slightly gashed. One man with a broken arm and another with a bad slash on his thigh. But we succeeded—the main enemy force is subdued."

"Good," Gaspar replied. "We're almost overdue to start. You know how demanding this next exercise is going to be. Leave behind anyone—*anyone*, man or beast—who you don't think is up to it."

That turned out to be five men and four horses, who were given instructions on how they could help with the third stage while everyone else mounted and formed up for this touchiest part of the action.

The ruse of the two 'scouts' had been to lure away and destroy a large portion of the enemy force. But there were still a dangerous number of marauders besieging the city, particularly near the gate. Alwenah's small army had been weakened by sending out about a third of their number under Captain Datis, and the remainder were now trapped within the city, no match for the army outside the walls. But if enough of the remaining enemy could be drawn off, those left at the city should be weak enough to be overcome by a sortie from the gates. The enemy knew this danger, and would be very cautious about sending too many of their fighters away. Any ploy to get them to commit more fighters had to be convincing enough to overcome that caution. That meant the ploy had to be dangerous, which was what the second stage of the evolution was about. This was why the best warriors had been kept back for this.

The last stretch of the road to Alwenah ran nearly due east, right toward the rising sun. It was up this road that Gaspar now led the company of horsemen, riding in close formation, toward the city gate. Hopefully the morning sun would bedazzle the enemy's eyes as they gazed down the road. Hopefully they'd mistake the horsemen for some of their own returning from battle. Hopefully the company would be allowed to get close enough before someone spotted that they weren't what they appeared.

That was a lot of hope for such a critical maneuver, but Gaspar knew that even Alexander had trusted to luck at times.

It took all Gaspar's nerve to hold his men in formation as they neared the enemy camp. The less they appeared to be an attacking force, the closer they'd get. He figured the enemy would be nervous and swift to respond to threats, but they'd also be anxious for any news of what was transpiring out in the valley. They'd cling to the slightest chance that the company might be their own men.

"Steady, men," Gaspar encouraged in a low voice. They were now half a mile from the enemy camp, and could smell the stench of smoking fires and camp latrines. Off to their right they could see a line of people chained together on the outskirts of the camp—Gaspar guessed that they were captives from Lur Dokis. They could see enemy soldiers watching them, some holding bows, but no alarm had yet been sounded and nobody was mounting up. Only a few hundred more yards to go—hopefully they could pull this off.

"Stand ready," Gaspar muttered, and the word was quietly passed back through the ranks. Gordias was riding to Gaspar's right and Tetius directly behind him. Neither had liked the idea of his riding point, but he trusted nobody else to call this action. Tigranes and the best archers were on the right side toward the rear, where they'd do the most good.

Just another furlong or so. Gaspar suddenly heard cries of surprise and alarm from the enemy camp. That was it—the marauders had finally discerned that the company wasn't their own. He could see them pointing and shouting and starting to scramble about.

"Now!" Gaspar cried, spurring his horse to a gallop. The company charged straight toward the enemy line, covering a furlong in short order. The marauders were now scurrying madly for their ponies. One archer who was on foot let fly an arrow that went wild and arced far overhead before dashing back into the camp.

That shot confirmed what Gaspar had been fairly certain of: they were now well within bowshot range. Now for their next tactic...

There they came: the pursuit, galloping out through the camp. "Turn!" cried Gaspar, pulling his horse to the left and galloping away across the valley. Behind him the company was drawing their bows and spreading out to afford the enemy a less concentrated target. Gaspar did not draw a weapon—he'd never mastered the lethal Parthian shot, fired backward from the back of a moving horse. His task was finding a sure road for the company to follow.

"Here they come," Gordias said. Gaspar's two men were now riding on either side of him.

"How many?" Gaspar asked.

"I'd guess five, maybe six dozen," Tetius replied after a pause.

Not so many as they'd hoped, but still a good number, and sure to be the cream of the remaining warriors.

"Arrows," warned Gordias, and the riders crouched down. The enemy was a couple furlongs back, well within range, and a flock of arrows dropped in their midst. None found a mark, and the company answered with a volley of their own. Gaspar didn't bother checking to see if their arrows were hitting. The galloping exchange of volleys was more to keep the enemy enraged and pursuing than to reduce their strength. Of far more interest to Gaspar was how distant the enemy was. His mind was racing—cavalry charges he was used to, but cross-country races while leading the enemy on was outside his experience. They had to keep a proper distance ahead—two furlongs was about right—but conserve enough of their horses' strength to put on a burst in the last half mile that would open another furlong. The archers would discourage the enemy from getting too close, but their horses' endurance was a different question.

"More arrows," Gordias warned again. There was a cry from behind, and Tetius looked back and cursed.

"One of ours?" Gaspar asked, and Tetius nodded grimly.

"Looks like an arrow caught his horse's right rear leg. The horse stumbled and threw him. Don't know who it was."

Gaspar winced. One of the accepted risks of this mission was no rescue. There was nothing for it—the company had to reach its goal no matter who fell along the way. His archers let off an answering volley—a cloud of arrows right into the enemy's face.

"That got at least three," Gordias said with dark satisfaction. Gaspar ignored him, focusing on the wagon track. It was leading in the right direction for now, but they may have to leave it soon. A mile gone already, less than three to go.

The deadly race pounded on. The marauders only fired one more volley before their bows fell quiet—they were learning that they came out on the worse end of arrow exchanges. Gaspar wondered when they would get curious about where they were being led at such high speed, and why they were following so blindly. Hopefully it wouldn't be for a little while longer. He peered ahead, scanning the rocky hills that formed the southwest wall of the valley. There it was, just as he'd been told: a smooth cliff with a wide reddish streak across the face. He turned slightly to aim for that. Less than two miles.

The ground began to rise. Gaspar could see the base of the cliff now. There they were— the rocks that marked the edge of the dry streambed. He had to take it on faith that the streambed was there. This was the only site he'd not been able to personally inspect last night. The hillmen had sketched and described it in detail, and it had sounded perfect for the purposes, so he'd drawn up his plan based on their description. He hoped the foot soldiers had made it into position, and had the long spears ready.

They were about half a mile from their goal now, the enemy still riding hard on their heels. With cries, Gaspar urged his horse to greater speed, and somehow the beast found it, laying his ears back and galloping just a little harder. The company followed suit, while behind them the enemy called in surprise and derision, wondering why their quarry was trying to run away faster. As they neared the ridge Gaspar began calling out the agreed password.

"Lur Dokis! Lur Dokis!" The company caught up the cry as they galloped over the ridge and down into the dry, sandy streambed.

The spearmen were there. The spears lay flat on the ground where they could be ridden over. The spearmen crouched low on the sides of the streambed, safely out of the way. When the last of the company had passed they dashed, still crouching, to the spears. Kneeling in the sand, hidden by the ridge, they awaited the foe.

They did not wait long. The marauders came hard on the heels of the company, charging recklessly up the ridge. "Now!" cried a watchman from a rock, and two dozen long spears rose from the streambed directly in the path of the galloping horses. The enemy had no time to turn or even to grasp what was happening. The front ranks were carried onto the bitter points by their own momentum, piling up in bloody, screaming chaos. The middle ranks crashed into them, adding to the confusion, but by now the cavalry company had dismounted from their exhausted horses and taken their bows to the top of some overlooking boulders. From this high ground they poured arrows into the ranks of the enemy at lethally short range. The foot soldiers were wading into the mayhem, laying about with swords and axes, crippling horses and pulling down riders to be dispatched on the ground.

It was over within five minutes. A handful of the rearmost horsemen managed to escape and flee in all directions, but most of the marauders lay slain or wounded. Having achieved nearly complete surprise, the valley defenders had sustained very few casualties. The stream bed and rise were soaked with enemy blood.

Gaspar and Tigranes met by their horses. "Victory, my lord," Tigranes said, saluting Gaspar.

"A hard won victory, at least here," Gaspar acknowledged. "Now it's up to Datis and his people back at the city."

As soon as the cavalry company had led most of the marauders off, hopefully to their deaths, Captain Datis slipped from hiding and ran to the rear wall of Alwenah. The city lay close to some outcroppings which afforded cover, where Datis had hidden during the night. His was the most simple, the most brazen, and one of the more dangerous missions of the day.

The first step was to alert the defenders inside the city. The skeleton crew of marauders that remained could not even patrol the city's exterior walls, much less encircle them, so they remained clustered near the gate. In their absence, Datis ran to within twenty yards of the wall and fired a few blunt arrows over it. Shortly one of the guards on the wall came over to see what the commotion was.

"Captain Datis!" the guard cried upon spotting him.

"Shh!" Datis urged. "Here—take this to the king." He fired one more arrow, this one with a message affixed to the shaft, then ran back to the cover of the rocks.

It took Datis half an hour to work his way back to where his men awaited him. There were only a dozen—all that could be spared given the needs of the other two sites—and they had all volunteered. They formed up, holding green-leafed branches in their hands, their swords remaining sheathed by their sides. Datis had the only spear, and he'd wrapped its head in a white scarf. He'd heard the Romans did that when indicating they had no intention of fighting, and though he doubted these barbarians were familiar with Roman customs, he hoped that the intent would be clear.

With jaw set Datis marched his men to the edge of the enemy camp. A row of the marauders stood staring at them. In the center of the row stood a slightly taller man with graying hair and bad teeth. He held a sword and was looking at them with naked hostility, but didn't appear to be attacking just yet.

"Do you speak our language?" Datis asked in Aramaic. The gray-haired man nudged a short, wiry warrior who stood next to him.

"I speak, some," the wiry man replied.

"I am Datis, captain of the army of Alwenah. I represent the king. I am ready to accept your surrender," Datis said slowly, allowing the man to translate as he spoke. At the end, the gray-haired man raised his eyebrows, gave an ugly smile, and said something in a tongue Datis did not recognize.

"My captain says you seem few and poorly armed for us to surrender to you," the wiry man translated.

Glancing beyond the gray-haired man, Datis replied, "You do not seem so many yourselves."

"When our troops return, we will be back to full strength. Then we will see who does the surrendering."

Datis licked his lips. This was the touchiest part—he hoped the king moved soon. "Your troops will not return. They have been vanquished by our army and our allies. You are all that remains of your army."

The gray-haired man snarled as this was translated. He brandished his sword and started to reply when there came cries and din from behind them. The marauders wheeled to see the city gates opening and defenders pouring out to confront the besiegers.

Datis let out a slow breath of relief, but held his place. Things were yet uncertain for him and his men—the battle could be won, yet they could still lose their lives.

The marauders watched for a minute as the city's troops moved through the camp, flushing the besiegers out of tents and camps. When they turned back, their faces were contorted with rage, but their eyes were filled with fear. Nervously the gray-haired man scanned the horizon for any sign of returning horsemen.

"They will not come," Datis said quietly. "They have fallen. But if you surrender to me, you will not be killed."

Upon hearing this translated, the gray-haired man's muscles tightened and his eyes glittered, but then his shoulders slumped in defeat. With a muttered oath he cast his sword on the ground, and his men followed suit.

"Run ahead," Datis commanded his men. "Tell them the marauders have surrendered and are to be treated as captives."

He turned to the gray-haired man. "Come—I will take you to my king."

It was a week later when the king of Alwenah, a fussy, nervous man named Mererdates, assembled his people for a solemn ceremony before the city's temple. The proper sacrifices were offered and litanies chanted. The three magi and their company were honored and thanked, especially Gaspar, who was awarded the title "Soter" (savior) and was made a perpetual noble of the city.

The week had been a busy one for all. The damage done by the marauders was repaired, largely by their efforts. A few hundred captives, mostly women and older children, were recovered from the marauders' camp. These were the only survivors of Lur Dokis, and had been destined for slavery either in their captors' homeland or at the markets of Hatra or Arbela. Now the marauders themselves met that fate, and the few who were not enslaved by citizens of Alwenah were dragged away to be sold. The caravan was generously reprovisioned and the lords laden with gifts. The three guards who had lost their lives were buried in honor, and three others who had been too wounded to continue the journey stayed behind to convalesce until they were well enough to return to the estate.

The temple ceremony was the farewell, and afterwards the caravan headed away from the city hailed by horns and cymbals and cheers.

"Well, then," Balthazar said to Gaspar as they rode toward the valley road. "I guess you're the hero of Alwenah."

"Tell that to the men we buried," Gaspar replied.

"There would have been many more, but for your inspired generalship," Balthazar reminded him. "That plan, drawn up that quickly under those conditions, was nothing short of genius. To conquer a superior force with such scant resources, using the terrain so effectively— Caesar himself would be proud! I'm surprised they didn't offer you the post of city general."

"Thank you. Actually, they did."

"Really? And you didn't accept?" Balthazar asked. "I'd have thought you'd jump at the chance to command your own army, even a small one."

"So did I," Gaspar admitted. "And I was certainly tempted, especially when the king outlined his plans. He intends to rebuild Lur Dokis, but as a secondary city, and to extend his kingdom to include both valleys. With that base for food and other resources, he hopes to build up his new, bigger kingdom's population so he can raise and train a proper army. For that, he needs an experienced general, and he asked me."

"Why didn't you accept the job on the spot?"

"A few reasons," Gaspar replied, as if he was still second-guessing his choice. "One was that I know where all this talk of more territory and a larger army usually leads."

"Designs on yet more valleys," Balthazar filled in.

"Exactly. And while sometimes that can work out, other times it can't—and here in Parthia it might mean eventually running afoul of the emperor. I think King Mererdates is better off running those risks by himself. Also, I know how the combination of an ambitious king and a successful general tend to work out. Either the general gets successful enough that he figures he should be king, or the king gets threatened enough that he removes the general. There's a fatality either way, and since I wouldn't do the former, I'd certainly fall to the latter."

"So," said Balthazar. "You passed up your chance for fortune, prestige, and a place in history as the rising general of Alwenah."

"Almost. I told the king I'd consider his offer, but I wanted to finish this journey first," Gaspar said, pulling a purse from his saddlebag. "At least I got the fortune part. The city fathers awarded me this in thanks for saving the city."

Balthazar gave a low whistle as he peered into the purse. "That's a lot of gold. You could retire on just that."

"I could," Gaspar admitted. "But I'd feel odd doing it. I strongly suspect this is plunder from Lur Dokis, retrieved from the marauders' camp. This gold has blood all over it. I just...don't know if I could use it."

"Offer some of it to a god," suggested Balthazar. "There are priests everywhere who'll say the purification rites over all of it for a donation of some of it. I know some in Hatra."

"Well...maybe," Gaspar said as he tucked the gold away. "And I'm not really worried about my prestige. As far as my place in history—if I have one, I hope it'll be because I pledged my sword to a worthier master than Mererdates of Alwenah."

HATRA

The High Priest Ushpiya descended the steps slowly. The request had been to meet him on the west staircase, which went from the torchlit upper courts down to the inky blackness at the temple base. He wasn't sure how far into that darkness he wanted to descend, not knowing exactly who awaited down there. He had his suspicions, but he still wasn't certain. It was concession enough that he was coming without his guard. This had better be worth it.

"That's far enough," came a rough whisper from behind a pillar to his right. The speaker was obviously trying to disguise his voice, but it wasn't working. Ushpiya recognized the voice and smiled. His suspicions had been correct.

"So," the High Priest replied, deciding to dispense with the pretenses. "I wondered if I'd be hearing from you."

"I…that is…thank you for coming," the voice said, though the speaker remained in the shadows. Clearly he hadn't expected to be recognized so easily.

"I imagine you're disappointed," Ushpiya continued in a sympathetic voice. "After all these years of service, to be passed over so callously."

"You…you know already?"

Ushpiya laughed. "You know how few secrets there are in Hatra. I knew when Pul took to his sick bed despite the temple's best efforts to keep it quiet. I knew when he summoned his

97

council. I knew what he'd announced while his successor was still vesting." He could have added that he'd known what the choice was before it had been made public, but there was no need to rub it in.

The voice cursed bitterly. Ushpiya sympathized—there could be only one high priest in any temple, and the post had gone to the voice's rival. But how to use this to his advantage? It depended on what the disappointed party wanted.

"So—what can I do for a priest of Atargatis?" Ushpiya continued.

"I was wondering…perhaps a place in your hierarchy?" the voice stammered.

So that was the direction. Difficult, desperate, almost hopeless—the competition in the temple of Nergal was at least as cutthroat as that in the temple of Atargatis. But that statement gave Ushpiya a clue as to how distraught the man was.

"You ask much," Ushpiya replied. "Many have devoted long years to Nergal's service, and worked hard to pass the levels of initiation." That was an argument the voice could sympathize with. "However, for those who have done Nergal some great service, some heroic deed, special…accommodation might be made."

"What kind of service?" the voice asked. Surely he'd expected something like this.

Ushpiya pondered only a moment. Why not reach high? In the end, this supplicant meant nothing to him. If he failed, the Temple of Nergal was out nothing. But if he succeeded…

"The Sapphire Crown," Ushpiya said decisively.

The voice gasped. "I…but…" it stammered.

"Atargatis has made plain what she thinks of your devotion. What do you owe her?" Ushpiya offered him some salve for his conscience.

"It…it will be difficult," the voice replied.

"That's your worry," Ushpiya answered bluntly. "That's the price of Nergal's help. Bring me the Sapphire Crown before the last day of the equinox festival."

There was a long silence before the voice answered quietly. "Very well. I will see what I can do."

"Don't bother coming back without it," Ushpiya replied. "Nergal has many priests who have already proven their devotion to him. As for those who speak without deeds—well, we have a few openings for acolytes." He turned and ascended the steps without looking back. After he had passed out of sight, a figure darted from behind the pillar and looked around, then descended to the base of the temple to disappear into the shadows.

"So," coaxed Gaspar. "Tell us about Hatra."

The caravan had been on the main road for about three weeks. Though they had fewer guards due to their losses at Alwenah, the ones they still had rode confidently, unconcerned about being accosted. Apparently a victory over a genuine army put road bandits into perspective. The men were certain they could manage whatever threat they might encounter. Now they were approaching their next major stop—the crossroads city of Hatra, which Melchior had never visited and Gaspar had only passed through a few times, never staying. Balthazar, however, knew Hatra well.

"You lived in Hatra for two years?" Melchior asked.

"Nearly three," Balthazar confirmed. "It was the closest I ever came to committing to a particular cult.

"Many roads lead to Hatra—the silk road from the Far East, the southeast road bringing travelers like us from Mesopotamia, the northwest roads bringing people from Anatolia and the Greek lands, and the southwest roads bringing traffic from Egypt and the Levant. Thus there are many merchants in Hatra, and much trading. Brokers who want the finest in eastern goods will linger in Hatra to snap them up, so they never even make it to Damascus or Antioch.

"As always where there are many travelers, there are many temples in Hatra. Those who have profited from a long journey and wish to offer thanks, those who are about to make a long journey and beseech favor, those with full pockets who wish to savor the pleasures certain temples offer—all can find a cult to suit them in Hatra. In fact, the Aramaic name for the city is House of God, and the great temple in the city's center is a sight to behold."

"With so much religious activity, I can see why you were drawn to it," Melchior said.

"Yes," Balthazar acknowledged. "I came there to learn and sample. I eventually settled in the Temple of Atargatis. The high priest was named Pul, and he was very fond of me. I also got along well with his two priests, Apiashal and Sanipu, and was particular friends with Sanipu. We studied together, and I learned the chief rites and incantations, and advanced to the threshold of the priesthood."

"In just three years?" Gaspar asked in amazement. "For most men that's a life of work."

"I'm a quick study, which was one reason they liked me. There are four stages of initiation into the cult, each stage with seven steps. I had learned the first stage at the Temple of Atargatis in Hierapolis, so when I walked into the temple in Hatra I was already an Initiate. I quickly passed through the Initiate steps and was a Temple Servant within a year. I'd made my way through the seven steps of the Temple Servant and was ready to enter into the next stage, Cleric, when I left."

"Why do that?" Gaspar asked. "After putting in so much effort and finding so much favor, why discard it just as the goal was coming into view?"

"That's what my friends wondered," Balthazar admitted. "And at times I wonder the same thing. Serving Atargatis suited me well, and I appreciated the devotion of her cult. But…I think we all have our place in the order of things, and our lives are spent searching for that place. I thought my place was at the altar of Atargatis, and so it may yet prove, but as the day of decision approached, I grew less certain. It seemed to my heart that I would be binding myself, trammeling myself too soon, were I to make that decision at that time. So I asked for a leave to further consider."

"How long ago was that?" Melchior asked.

"Almost four years. Pul let me go, but made me vow I'd give a definite answer to his face. I don't know if he's still alive to receive it, though—he was getting on in years even then. I think he'd hoped I'd be around to elevate to the full priesthood when he died, and one of his priests had to be appointed to the high priesthood. Apiashal and Sanipu got along as well as rivals for the same office ever could, but I could work with them both and sometimes acted as a peacemaker between them. I think it was Pul's hope that I'd be around when one of them was elevated, because there was certain to be hard feelings with the other."

"So, is this where we'll be staying, then? The temple, or a nearby inn?" Gaspar asked.

"No. The Temple of Atargatis has no accommodations for travelers, and we wouldn't want to stay at one of the inns, particularly a party of our size. I have a friend in Hatra, Shamshi-Adad, a trader in porcelains. He has a large house within the city and an estate outside it. At our last stop I sent a message ahead to him, so he should be expecting us."

Hatra was indeed impressive, with a long, high wall and many towers. But the streets were bustling and crowded, and the travelers were all tired, so they made no sightseeing stops other than to pass through the *temenos*, the sacred square, in the middle of the city. Balthazar pointed out the great temple dedicated to Samas the Sun God, as well as the temples of Atargatis, Allat, and Nergal. Then they went to the home of

Shamshi-Adad, who had gotten the message and was honored to host them. Arrangements were quickly made to quarter most of the caravan at his country estate, while the lords and a small retinue remained at the house in the city. Shamshi-Adad was beyond honored to house such dignified guests. The travelers were bathed and feasted and shown their host's exquisite collection of rare porcelains. They appreciated their airy sleeping chambers with the silken pillows, especially Melchior, whose older bones had been feeling keenly the rigors of so many weeks on the road. He and Shamshi-Adad were close in age, and shared a love of finer things, especially the rare teas of which Shamshi-Adad was a connoisseur.

The next morning Balthazar took Gaspar, Tigranes, and Baba down to the Temple of Atargatis. It was an impressive structure, with tall columns in the Greek style and lofty arches. Balthazar sent a message by a gate guard requesting permission to escort his guests around the temple to show them its glories.

"As with most temples, where you are permitted to go depends on your level of initiation into the mysteries of the goddess," Balthazar explained as they awaited a response. "As nonbelievers, you are permitted to enter the common court and worship there. Beyond that is the Court of the Devotees, where those who are receiving basic instruction are permitted. Within that court are the Chambers of the Initiates, open to the next level of worshippers. Since I have completed the third stage, you are permitted to go many more places in my company."

After a brief wait, they were amazed to receive their response not in the form of a response via messenger, but in the person of an elaborately robed man carrying a carved staff.

"Bithisarea!" the man cried. "Of all the events in these days, your arrival is the best omen yet!"

All the temple guards in the vicinity went down on one knee, so the travelers followed suit. The man lifted Balthazar to his feet.

"Apiashal! What an unexpected joy!" Balthazar said, then his brow furrowed and he gestured to the staff. "I see the high priesthood has passed on. It was well bestowed, but I mourn our father. How long has it been?"

"Just this past week we concluded the mourning rites," the priest explained. "He had hoped to see your face one more time before he died. But who are your companions?"

"Your Exaltedness, permit me to introduce Lord Gaspar, Captain Tigranes of our guard, and our aide Baba. We are on a journey from Seleucia on Eulaeus, and hope to tarry in Hatra for a time."

"You are welcome in the House of Atargatis, as all travelers are," Apiashal said. "I make you free of the temple while you are in the company of Lord Bithisarea, and will pass the word to the guards to permit your passage. The timing of your arrival is fortuitous—in a few days we will begin our autumn equinox festival, of which Bithisarea can tell you. In fact," he added with a sidelong glance at the Arabian. "With a brief purification rite, he is both qualified and welcome to serve at the ceremonies. The assistance would be appreciated."

With that, Apiashal returned to his duties, leaving Balthazar to show them the glories of the temple. Baba, and to some degree Tigranes, was awed at the size and magnificence of the edifice. Gaspar was less so, but even he had to admit that the rich gifts that adorned the temple walls were impressive by any standard.

"So, we're just in time for some great festival?" Gaspar asked.

"Atargatis is a goddess of order and harmony," Balthazar explained. "Neither too much nor too little—proper balance is her path. Scales, for instance, are under her authority. If there is drought or flood, or heat or cold, people appeal to her to restore balance. As such, the equinoxes, when day and night are equal, are the times when her power is at its peak. Week-long festivals are held leading up to each equinox, with rituals and ceremonies for each day, culminating on the equinox itself. On that day, the idol of Atargatis is brought out, richly robed and beautifully crowned, so that even the common devotees may see her. People are encouraged to ask favors when Atargatis is manifested on the equinoxes."

"Isn't she normally crowned?" Gaspar asked.

"She is, but I'm not allowed to speak of that," Balthazar replied. "But the equinoxial crowns are special, and worn only on that day for that ceremony. In the spring she wears a crown set with emeralds, symbolizing her dominion over field and harvest. For the autumn equinox, she wears a crown of sapphire, indicating her dominion over waters. The rest of the year her idol remains in the inner chamber, and is only seen by those who are at least initiates, and then according to specific protocols."

"So these equinoxial festivals are her major feasts?"

"There are other holy days, but those are the major ones. The court of devotees is jammed, and the outer court is crowded—everyone wants the favor of Atargatis on that day."

"And the High Priest wanted your assistance for the ceremony?" Gaspar said. "He must hold you in high regard."

"He does," Balthazar replied with a troubled look. "But even so, it was an unusual request. It makes me wonder if things are quite what they seem."

That question loomed so large in Balthazar's mind that after nightfall he made his way back to the temple by torchlight to request a private audience with the high priest. He was admitted to Apiashal's personal chambers to find a smiling but distraught looking host.

"Words cannot say how glad I am to see you, old friend," he said, handing Balthazar a cup of wine. "I meant it when I said that I consider your unexpected arrival a good omen, a sign that Atargatis favors my appointment."

"You had reason to doubt that?" Balthazar asked. Beneath the smiles, his friend looked haggard and careworn, aged much more than the passage of years could account for.

"Not really, but it's good to receive confirmation," Apiashal said, waving a hand. "Part of it has been the pressure of being high priest. Of course, we've both been taking on more of the day-to-day responsibilities during Pul's decline over the past year, but until the mantle descends on *you*, you don't appreciate just how hard it is. One thing I never grasped—old Pul did a good job of shielding us from it—is how brutal the competition is between temples here in Hatra. It's nothing he ever stooped to, and I hope not to, but some of these places are unscrupulous. They'll try anything to embarrass or shame or hinder someone else. As far as they're concerned, any setback by any other temple gives them a chance to advance.

"Then there's the burden of getting everything right. As a new high priest, every step I take is watched scrupulously. The least slip-up, the slightest bungling of some rite, is interpreted as a withdrawal of divine favor. It's already rumored that Pul's death just before the equinox is an ill omen, so I have to perform the ceremonies perfectly or the vultures will swoop."

"Isn't that something Sanipu could help with?" Balthazar asked.

An expression that looked like a mixture of anger and sadness flashed across Apiashal's face. He sighed and took a drink of wine.

"That's another thing that's been amiss of late. I knew that Sanipu would take it hard when I was elevated to the high priesthood over him. We both knew the day was coming, and we both knew that only one of us could be tapped. But I never guessed that he'd be so bitter. During Pul's funeral rites, he was only around for what he was absolutely required to attend. Since then, I've barely seen him. I presume he's executing his duties, but in truth, I've seen more of Sataspes, who was elevated to the

full priesthood to fill my spot, than I have of Sanipu. I don't
mean to speak ill of him, for I know how close you two were,
but I wish he was being more helpful."

"I love him like a brother," Balthazar admitted. "But that
doesn't make me blind to his faults. He always felt any slight
keenly, and had a long memory for grievances. But perhaps he's
still mourning Pul's death. He was like a father to him."

"He was like a father to us all", Apiashal said. "Perhaps you
can talk to Sanipu while you're here."

"Perhaps," mused Balthazar. Sensing that he wasn't helping
by lingering, he made his farewells, turning down the offer of an
escort back to the house. He lit his torch and stepped out into the
dark passageway. Something about the whole situation unsettled
him. Late though it was, he toyed with the thought of going down
to Sanipu's chambers to find out what he had to say. But even as
he gazed down the dark hallway in that direction, he heard a door
close and saw a dim figure slip through the shadows, heading
away from him.

"Sanipu?" Balthazar called tentatively. The figure stopped
briefly at the corner to glance back. It was too far for him to tell
for certain, but the face looked vaguely familiar. "Sanipu? It's
Bithisarea. Can we talk?" He started down the hallway, but the
figure slipped around the corner without saying a word or even
acknowledging the call. Balthazar stopped, mystified. Whoever
that was hadn't wanted to stop and talk, and Balthazar was
hardly going to chase him through the streets of Hatra. He
headed back to their lodgings, his heart heavy with concern for
his friends.

THE TEMPLE OF
ATARGATIS

The sun had set and the noise was rising around the temple of Atargatis. Balthazar and Gaspar were attending the first night of the equinox festival, which began when the sun dipped below the horizon. Melchior had elected to stay behind to savor the hospitality of Shamshi-Adad—something he had been doing a lot of during the four days they'd been here—but Tigranes had come along as understated security, since more than worshippers tended to show up for these major festivals. Baba had pleaded until Gaspar had granted him permission to tag along. Balthazar had conceded that seeing exotic temples and religious festivals could be part of the lad's education, but stated firmly that the first night was the only one he should attend. The rites of the later nights of the festival weren't suitable for young viewing.

"So, you didn't take your friend up on his offer to let you assist this week?" Gaspar asked Balthazar as they ascended the steps to the temple's main gate.

"No. The situation was—complicated," Balthazar replied. "Besides, that would have tied me to the temple through the upcoming week. Here, lad, keep close."

This admonition was to Baba, who was gazing around in wide-eyed wonder at the great court crammed with people. The air was heavy with smoke from the great bronze braziers that stood about the tops of the walls of the common court, flickering

107

with flames that were fed by temple attendants. Ceremonial drums pounded and people swayed and chanted. A platform had been erected at the end of the court near the gate that led to the Court of Devotees, and an altar had been set upon the platform, with a throne-like chair beside the altar.

"Every evening this week they'll have a ceremony out here, in the common court," Balthazar explained. "During the daytime there are various rituals and initiations at other places in the temple for people advancing through the levels. But most people come out to see this."

"Will we see your friend soon?" Baba asked.

"Apiashal? Not for a few hours yet. The junior priests do the early ceremonies. Each of these rites will last well into the night, and there are seven of them. He has to pace himself."

Some junior priests ascended the platform and began leading the congregation in chants of praise and supplication to Atargatis. Gaspar found the rhythmic pounding of the drums and the swaying of the worshippers working its way into his bones. Priests and temples and gods had never interested him much, but in this court he felt more keenly the tug of the transcendent, the lifting of the heart to something greater than itself. He found himself chanting along with the swaying men around him, men who suddenly seemed, if only for the evening, his brothers.

"Times like this," Gaspar commented to Balthazar. "Make me wonder if there might not be more to religion than I've given credit."

"We were in your world in the valley of Alwenah," Balthazar replied with a smile. "Welcome to my world. Entrancing in its way, but at least some of the expansive feelings can be traced to the herbs they mix in with the fuel they put in the braziers."

"Is that what that odd smell is?" Gaspar asked, shaking his head.

"Yes. Don't breathe too deeply, no matter what you see the people around you doing, or you'll have a ferocious headache in the morning."

Baba was already getting a bit of a headache, and was growing tired of the festivities. At first the grand building and flickering fires and exotic décor had interested him, but as more men crowded into the court, soon all he could see was shoulders of men a head or two taller than he. This was already becoming boring, and Lord Balthazar had hinted that it could go on all night! Baba began glancing around for opportunities to do what he did best—slip away and go exploring.

Just now, Lords Gaspar and Balthazar were talking and looking toward the front of the court. Captain Tigranes was scanning around for threats, as he always did, but there was already a man between them. Baba unobtrusively backed away until it was two men, and then three, and then he was out of the captain's view, lost in the crowd. No matter—he was good at finding people again, and Captain Tigranes was easy to spot. He'd just have a look around this imposing temple and be back before they knew he was gone.

There was still a good amount of traffic coming through the main gate, so Baba was able to slip out without being noticed. He didn't want to go back out into the dark streets of Hatra, but the temple grounds were ample for exploring. There was a perimeter wall that clearly wasn't intended to stop anyone—it was only waist-high on Baba. Temple guards were stationed along this wall at wide intervals, armed with shields and spears and looking bored. Baba guessed that their role was more to guide strayed worshippers and revelers back to the festivities than to actually guard anything. Still, they could cause him some problems, so he hugged the main temple wall. There were about twenty yards of open grounds between the perimeter and the temple wall, and he was accustomed to moving quietly. The guards shouldn't hear him.

Baba slipped along the wall, masked by shadows cast from the flaming braziers overhead. This wall had the most interesting feature—insets fronted by columns, and occasionally short corridors that ran behind façade walls. It seemed like the temple wall was constructed to allow people to pass along it then duck behind something that would mask where they were actually entering the building. Once or twice he thought he saw an opening to his left, the mouth of some corridor that led into the temple. He wondered if he'd have the courage to try any of those dark portals.

Baba had made his way along nearly the full length of the main wall, and was approaching the corner, when he heard the noises. The din of the common court had faded to a distant roar, and the scant light from the braziers had long since been left behind. Baba was ghosting along in silence by the light of a half moon, keeping himself hidden behind what columns he could find. From the darkness ahead he heard noises that stopped him in his tracks— the muffled but distinctive sound of men struggling. Someone was grunting and panting, and there was the clear sound of something striking metal. It didn't sound like an open fight—there were no cries or sharp sounds—so Baba wondered if it was several men overpowering another. It seemed like someone was going out of their way to keep the scuffle quiet.

Baba was very frightened. He knew he was on shaky ground, having slipped away without permission to explore these forbidden temple grounds. Now it sounded like he'd stumbled upon something truly dangerous in the shadowy darkness. He had to get away from here, quickly, or he might be caught up in the trouble, maybe even blamed for it! But what could he do? If the past few weeks had taught him anything, it was that grownups could do some truly horrible things. He had to tell someone about these ominous noises, but who? Not the temple guards—they'd arrest him for being where he shouldn't be. Who?

Lord Balthazar! He had some official status about the temple. He'd know what to do. Baba listened carefully. The muffled sounds had fallen silent, which worried Baba more, and lent a sense of urgency. Moving with more caution and quiet than he'd ever mustered, he backed away and fled into the shadows, quickly retracing his steps along the wall.

The common court was more crowded and smoky than ever, but Baba slipped through the bodies unnoticed. He found the adults standing roughly where he'd left them, apparently having never noticed his absence. Mustering his courage, he tugged on Lord Balthazar's sleeve.

"Oh, hello, Baba," Lord Balthazar said with a smile. "How are you liking the festival?"

Baba swallowed and realized that he was going to have to confess to slipping away in order to convey his news, but there was no option.

"Lord Balthazar, sir, something's wrong. Men fighting in the dark toward the back of the temple."

Balthazar's brow furrowed in alarm and Tigranes, who'd leaned over to listen, asked, "What fighting, lad? What darkness?"

"Here, let's get over here where it's quieter," Balthazar pulled Baba behind a pillar. All three men listened as Baba recounted in guilty detail everything about his slipping away and what he'd heard. He better understood how foolish he'd been when he saw how Lord Balthazar's eyes widened and lips tightened when he told of his escapades. When he'd finished, Lord Balthazar put his big right hand on Baba's shoulder, forcing him to look full into his eyes.

"What you did was very dangerous, Baba. These are not the estate stables. You should never go anywhere on these grounds without an adult, preferably me. Do you understand?"

"Yes, sir," Baba mumbled sheepishly.

"But you were right to bring this to me. Describe again what you heard in the darkness."

So Baba did, trying hard to remember every detail. Then the three men stepped away to confer before returning.

"Baba, Lord Gaspar is going to take you home. I'm sure I don't have to tell you to remain right by his side," Lord Balthazar said.

"No, sir," Baba replied.

"Very well. Tigranes, if you would come with me."

"Yes, sir."

They made their way back to the main gate, where Gaspar took Baba away while Balthazar and Tigranes started walking around the perimeter wall. They came to the first guard, who saluted them. They continued along the perimeter, watching all around as they proceeded.

"The lad's a handful," Tigranes said. "Though he may have stumbled onto something useful tonight."

"Yes," Balthazar replied with a concerned look. "He'd been frightened enough already, so I didn't want to point out to him that he'd been toying with death. Even Initiates aren't allowed to wander near the temple walls."

"These guards seem rather—widely spaced," Tigranes observed as they approached the next guard station.

"They are," Balthazar explained. "During the festival, most of the guards are inside to watch the crowds. The newer, less experienced guards man the perimeter."

"Do you think Baba heard something sinister?" Tigranes asked.

"Perhaps," Balthazar replied guardedly. "But there are some things I want to check before sounding an alarm. It's possible that he heard something that would be…expectable—only I wouldn't look for it on a festival night."

Tigranes said nothing, thinking of Baba's description of what he'd heard and wondering for what kind of operations such sounds would be 'expectable'. He strongly suspected that Balthazar knew things about the operations of temples that weren't widely discussed. They walked along through the dimness, passing a couple more guards before Balthazar began to slow down and look about suspiciously.

"Spot something?" Tigranes asked.

"It's what I haven't spotted—we should have encountered another guard by now. Come on, let's go a little further."

They went another fifty yards or so before Balthazar stopped again, clearly agitated. "Something's definitely wrong. We should have reached another guard along this stretch. Do you have your flint and tinder?"

"Always, sir."

"Come on, then," Balthazar turned toward the temple wall. They reached it and began groping along its length.

"To think Baba could have made his way along here," Tigranes said.

"Young eyes," Balthazar said. "Ah, here's a pillar."

"What are we looking for?"

"Torches. They keep them stored about the grounds, usually strapped to the backs of pillars or on shelves in walls. Here we go. Your flint, please?"

The two men soon were walking slowly through the shadows, looking about warily. Balthazar seemed to know what he was looking for, holding his torch high and feeling along the wall. They were near the corner, behind one of the short freestanding walls situated a few feet from the main wall, when Balthazar turned left into a dark doorway, then took a sharp right, and then another left. Tigranes followed and found himself stepping into a moderate sized chamber that had a musty barnyard smell. Along the far wall a ledge made of stone blocks stood out from the wall about four feet, making a shelf that stood waist height extending nearly the entire length of the wall. At one end of this ledge another stone construct about five feet wide stuck three feet further into the room. There were torch brackets on the walls and iron rings set into the stones, including along the face of the ledge and around the stone construct.

In the middle of the floor lay the bodies of two temple guards, both with their throats cut and their blood covering the floor.

Tigranes breathed in sharply while Balthazar surveyed the scene with grim eyes. There was no need to ask if this had been expected.

"Tigranes, go find the nearest guard. Have him find Apiashal and tell him to come to the east sacrifice holding chamber. Bid him come by the Ring of Ipsus."

"The Ring of Ipsus. Yes, sir," Tigranes said, then ducked out. While he was gone Balthazar found and lit more torches, moving about the edge of the chamber so as not to disturb the bodies or the scant dust on the stone floor. Tigranes returned presently, and Apiashal arrived shortly thereafter. He was dressed in a ceremonial robe and had the look of one who had been interrupted in preparations. He came with guards, but left them outside, entering the chamber and beholding the scene with a mixture of shock and horror.

"We got word of a disturbance along the east temple wall toward the rear," Balthazar explained. "We went around the perimeter wall and found at least two of the guards missing. This being the closest chamber, I looked in here and found this. We have left everything as we found it, except that I lit the torches about the walls."

Apiashal took this in while looking at the bodies, at Balthazar, and at the stone ledge along the far side of the chamber. "This," he finally said, "is a terrible act of defilement. To shed the blood of temple officers, within the temple precincts, during the festival, even while the worship was taking place—this is unforgiveable. Atargatis will demand a terrible accounting for this desecration."

"Do you have any idea who might have done this? Or why?" Balthazar asked.

Apiashal glanced at the stone ledge, then at the two dead men. "I have my suspicions about both, but no way to prove it yet."

"Why is one of the guards lacking a helmet?" Tigranes asked. Both of the bodies wore temple livery, but one's helmet was missing—not just knocked off his head, but nowhere to be seen. The other guard still wore his helmet.

"I don't know, Captain, but again, I have my suspicions," Apiashal replied, beginning to walk about the bodies. "His spear is also missing, I notice. I wonder, I wonder..." he glanced again at the stone ledge.

"Should we get the guards searching the grounds?" Balthazar asked. "Whoever did this could not have gone far in this brief time."

"Yes, the brief time," Apiashal muttered. "Bithisarea, your summons was most timely. I suspect that we shall not have to search the grounds, for those who did this will not have gone far. But there is one thing I must check to be certain. Gentlemen, would you turn your backs for a short while?"

Balthazar and Tigranes did so, and heard nothing but Apiashal moving about the room and muttering to himself. After a time he said, "Thank you, gentlemen. You may turn around now." This they did, to find the high priest standing between the bodies of the guards, his expression a mixture of simmering rage and grim satisfaction.

"Yes, my friend, your summons was timely indeed. In fact, you may have averted a great catastrophe."

"You mean—greater than this?" Balthazar indicated the two bodies on the ground.

"Amazingly, yes. As you know, this chamber is used as a staging room for sacrificial animals being brought up to the altar. But it is more than that. One of the rings is a pin. If you tug on it firmly, it comes out of the wall." He gestured toward the stone construct that stood out from the ledge. "That pin is now missing from its place.

"Only the full priests of Atargatis know that pin is there, and what it is for. This structure," he patted the stone ledge, "is not just for tying up livestock and piling bales of hay. This holds an opening mechanism with a counterweight on one end." He pointed toward the far end of the ledge. "And a door at the other," he pointed to the stone construct. "This door looks like plain stone blocks, but if the pin is removed, it doesn't take much leverage to lift the face and expose the passageway that lies behind it."

"A passageway that leads to…?" Balthazar asked.

"The secondary treasure chamber."

"Secondary treasure chamber? I didn't know there was a secondary treasure chamber."

"Most people don't," Apiashal explained. "Like you, most people only know the main treasure chamber on the second level—the one with the prominent doors and elaborate locks and constant guards. We do keep treasure there, but it's mainly showy but relatively trivial things such as ceremonial robes and hangings. We leave a few chests of gold and smaller jewels around for appearances, but for most of the year the highly valuable goods are stored here."

"Ah," Balthazar nodded. "So that if thieves do manage to penetrate the safeguards around the main chamber, all they'll be able to reach is the goods of lesser value."

"Precisely," Apiashal confirmed. "Which was what mystified me. Whoever would know that this treasure chamber is here would also know that it is nearly empty. Just before the two major festivals, most of the contents of this chamber are brought to the main chamber for easy access during the ceremonies. For the past weeks I've been discreetly moving things upstairs in preparation. Right now, the chamber is almost empty, except for—"

"The crowns," Balthazar guessed.

"Exactly," the high priest confirmed. "The two crowns are too precious to have lying around, so they stay in there until the nights they are needed."

"They aren't sitting out in the open down there, are they?"

"No—there are corners and hidden closets even there. Nothing to foil a determined thief, but enough to delay him. Which may have proven sufficient, given your timely warning, Bithisarea."

"But—aren't you concerned?" Balthazar was puzzled by Apiashal's apparent inaction. "Do you think the crowns have been stolen?"

"Actually, I think they *are* being stolen. I think we've caught the thieves in mid-theft."

"So...you mean..." Tigranes asked, pointing at the stone structure.

"Exactly, Captain. I think the intruders are in the chamber right now, possibly listening to us, if they can hear through that stone. I don't know, I've never tried."

"How can you tell?" Balthazar asked with a puzzled scowl.

"I can't be sure, but I'm fairly certain. For one thing, the pin's gone. If I were down there, I'd want the pin with me to insure nobody put it back. For another, a helmet and spear are gone. They probably used the helmet as a fulcrum and the spear handle as a lever to lift the door; they'll need them again to get out. I'm guessing that if they'd finished and gone, the pin would be in place, that guard's helmet and spear would be back, and we'd be left with a mystery—and some missing crowns. No, my lord, I'm guessing your summons came at just the right time."

"So—should we open the door? Or catch them coming out? Should I send for more guards?" Balthazar asked.

"No, no more guards," Apiashal said. "The location of this entrance is a closely guarded secret—we don't want to let more people in on it."

"But...then...," Balthazar stammered, even more puzzled. "You don't think we three could face...we don't know who or how many are down there!"

"I'm sure that there aren't many—just enough to overpower the guards," Apiashal replied. "As far as who—I've got a good guess, and I think you do, too, Bithisarea."

Balthazar scowled, then his eyes grew wide. "Surely you don't think..."

"I don't know what to think," Apiashal said in a sad voice. "But I know this temple can't stand a major scandal right now, and this would be a major scandal. The question is, what to do about it?"

Apiashal stood pondering while Balthazar and Tigranes looked at each other in shock. Balthazar thanked Baba in his heart, and resolved to slip the sneaky little rascal a coin at the next opportunity. But something was nagging him, something tied to what Apiashal had just said—what was it?

"Ah," the high priest said. "I think I have a solution." He picked up the remaining spear and, with some effort, broke the handle using one of the rings in the wall. "If you two would be kind enough to turn your backs again for a moment?" This they did, and all they could hear was Apiashal being busy at one end of the room.

"Thank you," he said, and they turned around to see him coming back toward the center of the room.

"Can you tell us what you did?" Balthazar asked.

"Not in detail, but in light of your assistance, I can let you know that there's more than one secret in this room. The party after the crowns, the one who is probably down in the treasure chamber right now, knew about the pin that locks and releases the door. But there is another spot where a stick of a certain length inserted into a particular hole will jam the counterweight. As long as that stick is in place, the door will never lift."

"So they'd be—"

"Trapped down there," Apiashal interrupted. "That's the beauty of it. If I'm wrong, and there's nobody down there, then no harm. But if I'm right, and there are murdering thieves in the chamber—well, justice will be swiftly and aptly served."

Balthazar and Tigranes were both aghast at the cold-blooded manner in which Apiashal said this.

"But...with no food or water, they'll die in three days!" Balthazar cried.

"I'll give them four, just to be certain."

"Apiashal, you must know who's down there," Balthazar grabbed his arm. "You can't do that to him! He was your friend!"

"Can't I? Yes, he was my friend, and I was willing to be his. But if he uses the secrets he's learned to murder and plunder and disgrace this temple, then he's no friend of mine—and he deserves to end like this!"

There it was again—that thing that had been nagging Balthazar, only this time he caught it. Cold panic seized his insides. He motioned Tigranes to step over near the doorway while he urged Apiashal to the far side of the room.

"You are throwing temple secrets around rather casually, old friend, considering present company," Balthazar said in a low voice.

"Bithisarea, you have my complete trust, especially considering what you have just saved us from. You have nothing to worry about."

"I'm not the one I'm worried about," Balthazar replied, discreetly nodding toward Tigranes. Apiashal gave a glance and a small shrug.

"Apiashal, he's not even my servant—he's faithfully served my colleague for many years. He's also my friend."

"It cannot be helped," Apiashal said. "As you well know, even Initiates don't know this chamber exists, much less its secrets. That man isn't even a Devotee, but an unbeliever. His life is forfeit for even being here."

"He was here at *my* request, helping *me* solve a terrible problem for *you*. It is not his fault that he has learned temple secrets!" Balthazar replied, panic warring with fury.

"I know that, but he cannot leave knowing what he knows. Even if he was confined to the temple grounds for the rest of his life, he might still speak to someone. I'm sorry, but it cannot be otherwise. You should be able to find another servant with little trouble—the temple will reimburse you for the cost."

Balthazar ground his teeth, frantically searching for options. "Apiashal, he is under my protection! Would you see my word violated?"

Apiashal spread his hands. "You know full well that there are rules that bind even the high priest. I am helpless in this matter."

"You are not helpless!" Balthazar replied in a sharp whisper. "All you have to do is not give the order! None of this is his fault, and he should not die for it! He is as innocent as your guards lying there with their throats slit! Listen—listen—what if he were to give you his solemn oath? He is an honorable man. If he gave his bound word, he would keep it until death. Would that satisfy you?"

"The word of an unbeliever? By what could he swear that would matter to me?"

"The man is not godless. He is a Jew. The second of their Great Commandments forbids them to falsely invoke the Name of their God. If he were to take a vow by that Name to never come here again, nor to communicate to any man by any means what he has learned of this chamber, would that suffice? I know

Jews, and they guard such oaths with their lives. It would keep him silent every bit as well as killing him."

Apiashal looked at him shrewdly. "I have known some Jews in my day as well." Then his expression softened. "Your devotion to this man is to your credit, Bithisarea. As you know, we need priests of such devotion here—all the more so now." He glanced at the door to the treasure chamber. "If I grant you this, will you consider returning to Atargatis to undertake her service once again?"

"Yes, I will seriously consider it."

"Very well. Let us see about a vow from your Jewish servant."

They stepped over to Tigranes, where Balthazar explained the severity of the situation, leaving out the part about the automatic death sentence. Tigranes nodded gravely, being familiar with such security measures and understanding the need for secrecy.

"And so," Balthazar concluded. "The high priest has graciously agreed to accept your solemn oath to never come here again, nor to speak of or make known in any way the existence or secrets of this chamber. Are you willing to so swear by the holy Name of your God?"

Tigranes bowed to Apiashal. "I thank the high priest for his most gracious clemency in this matter, especially for one who is not of his cult. I know the high priest holds my life in his hands, and if he is willing to accept my oath, I can only be grateful."

Apiashal nodded. "Now make your oath."

Tigranes pondered for a minute. Balthazar understood his quandary. His oath had to be properly worded to satisfy Apiashal, and had to be in the name of his God. But he could not vow by the name of Atargatis, who was in his tradition a false goddess. He had to figure out some way to give the oath validity in the eyes of the temple.

Tigranes lifted his head and drew his dagger. Walking over to where the two guards lay dead, he nicked the edge of his hand. Holding out his hand so his dripping blood fell to mingle with the blood on the floor, he spoke.

"I solemnly vow by *Hashem*, the Holy Name, to never come to this chamber again, nor to speak to any man of its existence, nor to write or draw, nor to communicate to any man, living or yet unborn, by word or deed, by action or inaction, that I know anything of the Temple of Atargatis outside of the common court. This vow I hold until death, by *Hashem*, the Holy Name."

Clever Tigranes, thought Balthazar. He had not invoked the name of Atargatis, but by mingling his blood with that of the men who had died in the service of her temple, he had created a powerful bond. But how would Apiashal respond?

The high priest pondered and then nodded. "By the Third Secret Name of Atargatis I accept your oath, and in that name I release you from the usual penalty for knowing of this chamber. May your oath bind you to death, and if you fail of it, may the curse of Atargatis and your god strike you wherever you are and visit that same fate upon you and your posterity." He pointed toward the bodies on the floor.

"So be it, by *Hashem*." Tigranes agreed. Balthazar pulled out a kerchief and bound his hand, while Apiashal summoned in the guards who had been standing just outside the door. They began to carry out the bodies while Balthazar hustled Tigranes away.

"I hope that doesn't fester," Balthazar said as they made their way through the darkened streets.

"I keep my blades clean," Tigranes assured him.

"How quickly can you pack?"

"My lord, I'm a soldier. I can be ready to go in ten heartbeats."

"Good, because you're going to need to. The house is just ahead—I won't even come in. Gather your gear, get your horse, and meet me at the front gate."

Tigranes, accustomed to obedience, was back out on the street within minutes of their arrival at the house.

"Where are we going, my lord?" Tigranes asked as he led his horse behind the hurrying Balthazar.

"We're getting you out of the city. Every hour you stay increases your danger."

"But—I don't understand. The high priest swore I was safe-released from the penalty."

"The high priest forgets what a good student I am," Balthazar replied. "By their own teachings, a vow made to a nonbeliever is not binding. Even oaths made to their own devotees are only considered valid under certain circumstances. I suspect he said what he did to mollify me, and get out of a difficult situation. He reasoned that it would be easier to let you go now and send an agent after you later. Hatra is full of men who will do such a deed for a small purse of silver. By sunset tomorrow your boots would be worth more than your life within the city walls.

"I'm taking you to the main city gate. Listen to me now and obey these instructions. Ignore whatever I say at the gate, that will be for the benefit of the guards. I want you to ride tonight toward Duro-Europa, but don't head there directly. Initially, ride east until you are out of sight of the city gates. Then cut across country until you rejoin the western road. Once you get to Duro-Europa, hide among your own people. There is a synagogue there. Do not let your name be used—if possible, find another.

"That will be easy—I'll just use my Hebrew name," Tigranes said.

"Can you tell me what it is?"

"Oh, it's no secret, my lord. Among my people I am known as Yusef."

"Very well. When we reach Duro-Europa, we will ask for you among the Jews by that name. But Tigranes should vanish until we are beyond Damascus. The Temple of Atargatis in Hatra has long arms, reaching from Ctesiphon to Tarsus. But here is the gate."

"Won't it be closed for the night?" Tigranes asked.

"Some keys open all doors," Balthazar said, jingling a purse. He had Tigranes stay back while he did some negotiating with the gate guards, and then came back for him while one of the guards opened a postern gate.

"I've hinted that you got yourself in trouble with some of the temple women, and are being sent home in disgrace," Balthazar explained. With some careful stepping they got Tigranes' horse out through the guardhouse. Outside the gate, under the eye of a guard, Balthazar slapped Tigranes on the shoulder and pressed the purse into his hand.

"Here, this should get you to Ctesiphon," he said in a slightly raised voice. "Contact your master's agent there for further funds—and try to stay out of trouble, if you can."

"Yes, my lord," Tigranes replied with just the right note of sheepishness. He mounted and rode off through the night while Balthazar returned through the postern gate, muttering something about country boys and big cities.

Back at the house the lords held a hurried torchlit conference. Balthazar explained that due to some trouble at the temple about which he could not speak, he'd had to send Tigranes on ahead, and they all needed to leave Hatra as soon as feasible. What with advancing the provisioning efforts and getting the men prepared, that looked to be about three days hence. The next morning, Balthazar summoned Baba and instructed him that he had never wandered away the night before, hadn't heard any noises in the dark, and had stayed by their sides in the common court for the whole evening. In short, he had not seen, heard, or known of anything amiss at the Temple of Atargatis.

On the morning they left Hatra, the magi stopped at the temple where Balthazar sent a message by one of the guards notifying Apiashal of their departure. To their surprise, they were asked to await the high priest's response. To their even greater surprise, the high priest came out to respond in person, accompanied by a slave carrying an ornate wooden box.

"Your Exaltedness honors us," Balthazar said, bowing at the high priest's approach.

"The Temple of Atargatis is honored by the visit of sages of such repute," Apiashal replied. "Lord Melchior, I presume? We have not met, yet your renown as a scholar and wise man precedes you. Even here in Hatra princes and wealthy merchants boast of having a horoscope that was cast by you."

"Your Exaltedness is too kind," Melchior said with a bow.

"Am I correct that you are traveling without the captain of your guard?" Apiashal asked, his eyes glancing over the small company.

"We received a message from home requiring him to return there," Melchior explained.

"Indeed," the high priest replied, his eyes flicking to Balthazar. "But I could not let you leave without properly thanking the Lord Bithisarea, who recently rendered a service of inestimable value to Atargatis."

The other lords looked inquisitively at Balthazar, who shrugged. "It was nothing I could speak of."

"Sadly true, but that does not make the service any less valuable. As a token of her gratitude, Atargatis wishes to give Lord Bithisarea this gift." Apiashal opened the box and lifted out a richly embroidered bag. Balthazar stepped forward to accept it, and Apiashal added in a lower voice, "I hope the Lord

Bithisarea will consider carefully his promise, and remember that Atargatis can always use leaders of his caliber."

"I shall," Balthazar replied quietly, taking the bag, which gave off a rich aromatic scent. "For my part, I ask your Exaltedness to remember that it has not yet been three days. I offer all this back to the goddess if you will reconsider your decision." He held the bag out to Apiashal.

The high priest closed his eyes as pain passed across his face, but when he reopened them they were hard. He pushed the bag away and shook his head. Balthazar nodded and turned to go.

"May Atargatis guide and guard your journey," Apiashal pronounced formally, raising his arms. They bowed again as he turned and returned to the temple.

"What did he give you?" Melchior asked as they turned toward the city gates.

Balthazar opened the bag, sniffed it, and handed it to Melchior. "Frankincense."

"A good amount of it, too," Gaspar said in wonder. "That must be three or four pounds. That's a small fortune—the Romans pay handsomely for that to use in their pyres."

"Yes," mused Balthazar glumly. His sleeping and waking hours had been tormented by imaginings of what was transpiring in the dry darkness beneath the temple. He'd tried to console himself with the hope that Apiashal had been mistaken, that there was nobody behind that stone door. But he had to admit that it was at least equally likely that there was. He would never know for certain.

"An interesting payment," Gaspar said. "Why not just give you gold? Incense is the sort of thing that's taken into temples, not out of them."

"It has cultic significance," Balthazar explained. "It's been offered to Atargatis, so if I burn a pinch of this while appealing to her, it'll be just like the high priest was offering the prayer in person at the altar here in Hatra. It's the greatest gift the high priest can offer."

"I see," said Gaspar. "It's more than just the value of the frankincense, it's the fact that it's been offered to a god. It's like you're carrying a little temple to Atargatis with you everywhere you go."

"Right. Could—you hold that for me?" Balthazar asked when Melchior tried to return the bag of incense. "I don't wish to carry it just now."

JERUSALEM

"What's that, Tigranes?" Gaspar asked. It was later afternoon and the sun was falling toward the horizon. They'd just passed a bend in the road that had brought them within sight of their destination: the ancient city of Jerusalem. The fading sunlight illuminated the city, seeming to bathe it in gold, and Tigranes had muttered something audible yet incomprehensible to Gaspar, who spoke many tongues.

"I'm sorry, my lord," Tigranes apologized. "I was using the speech of my fathers, Hebrew, to say a song of ascending. It is customary for pilgrims to recite them along the road as they drew near the temple. Roughly translated, it says:

Those who put their trust in the Lord are like Mount Zion, unshakeable, and will abide forever.
As the hills stand all about Jerusalem, so the Lord stands about His people, now and for days to come.

The caravan's journey from Hatra had been uneventful, if wearying. They'd passed through Duro-Europa, where they'd picked up Tigranes without incident, and had proceeded through Damascus and down through the region of the Galil, a rich farming area. Tigranes had explained that this land had once belonged to the Israelites, but that it had been conquered centuries before by other nations. Now under Roman jurisdiction, the area was at peace, and the travelers found their

129

situation inverted. While traveling in the East, the long empty roads had been the danger zones and the cities havens of safety. Here in the Levant, the well-policed roads were safer than the bustling cities crowded with opportunists of all types. They were certainly back within the sphere of the Roman *Mare Nostrum*, a world more familiar to Gaspar and Balthazar than to Melchior and most of his household.

Tigranes was the exception to that. "How many times have you been to Jerusalem, Tigranes?" Gaspar asked.

"This will be my third time, my lord. My first time was shortly after I'd come of age. My uncle was making a pilgrimage, and my parents allowed me to come. The other time was about eight years after that. Both times were for the Feast of Weeks—Pentecost as the Greek-speakers call it. Someday I hope to be here for Passover, the great feast."

"Is that the protocol? There are particular seasons for pilgrimage?"

"All Jews hope to come to Jerusalem someday, no matter the season," Tigranes explained. "But there are three great feasts in the year: Passover, the Feast of Weeks, and the Feast of Booths. These are all prescribed in our sacred writings. There are other, lesser traditions which we also celebrate."

"Will any of these be going on while we're visiting?" Gaspar asked.

"No, thankfully, otherwise there wouldn't be room for us. As it is, I'm sure I can find somewhere. I asked around in Duro-Europa and got some names to look up."

The caravan soon called a halt and pitched camp in a nearby field, judging the distance to Jerusalem too long to cover in what remained of the day. Tigranes was sent riding ahead to hunt up lodging for their arrival the next day while the three magi conferred over supper. Balthazar, being the resident expert on religions and cults, did most of the talking.

"I've never been to Jerusalem," he admitted. "Though it's the center of Judaism, they only have one temple, and their priesthood is a hereditary affair not open to outsiders. In fact, there isn't much about the Jews that's open to outsiders, especially here in their home nation of Judea. To them, the world is divided into themselves, the Circumcised, and the rest of us, the Uncircumcised. That's not exactly accurate, since other peoples circumcise, but to the Jews, circumcision is the ritual for men to enter the covenant with their God. So it's really a way to differentiate between those in the covenant and those without. Be prepared—they can be a little prickly about non-Jews, particularly in their Holy City."

"Their animosity is somewhat understandable," Gaspar added. "Given that the Syrian Greeks tried to wipe them out a few generations back."

"There is that," Balthazar admitted. "Point being, we're going to want to visit the temple, which is apparently quite a sight—their king rebuilt it not long ago, and it's impressive— but we'll have to be careful where we go. Non-Jews are allowed some places but not others, and the Jews are very touchy about where."

"Like some other temples we've been to recently, eh, Balthazar?" Gaspar ribbed.

"What about this king?" Melchior asked. "What do you know of him?"

"Not much," Balthazar admitted. "His name is Herod, and he likes to build things. Aside from the temple he also built Caesarea Maritima on the coast and some other forts. Like many kings in this part of the world, he likes to impress with architecture. Gaspar may be able to tell you more than I."

"Not much more," Gaspar said with a shrug. "This Herod was apparently embroiled in Antony and Cleopatra's machinations out here in the east, but came out on the right side of it all—the Roman Senate appointed him King of the Jews."

"The Roman Senate?" puzzled Melchior. "What would they—no matter. What manner of man is he? Do you think he'll be offended that we showed up so late to honor his son's birth?" "I've no idea," Balthazar said. "Some of these petty kings can be touchy, but I hope he would understand given the distance we had to travel. And I don't know of any king who'd turn down the kind of gifts we've brought."

The next morning Tigranes returned, having found sufficient lodging for the entire caravan. The host, one Yochanan, was related to the Sadducees, and thus could house *goyim*. Apparently many of the lodgings in Jerusalem followed the teachings of the Pharisees, who would not have non-Jews stay under their roof. Much of this was lost on the magi, who were just glad to have a place to stay. Furthermore, Yochanan had connections at court, so Tigranes had asked him to start looking into securing an audience with the king.

The lords took their time getting ready that morning, setting aside their dusty travel clothing and arraying themselves in finer garb—not their court wear, but capes and turbans dyed and decked in the style common to the East. Tigranes had the guards tidy and polish their gear, and even Baba was given a bright scarlet cloak and a headband sparkling with polished quartz. The caravan was quite the sight as it approached the gates of Jerusalem, with Tigranes leading the guards in close formation, the magi riding in colorful splendor, and the laden camels following. Crowds parted for them and rumors rippled through the streets of the Parthian noblemen who had arrived. Jerusalem was long accustomed to Jews of all types: poor Jews, rich Jews, martial Jews, influential Jews, Jews from down the road and across the world all entered through her gates. But these exotic Gentiles, neither customers nor conquerors, were a novelty that set tongues wagging.

Tigranes led the small parade to the house of Yochanan, who met them at the gate with low bows. He also was impressed with the pomp, and was keenly conscious of the reputation his house would gather by hosting such guests. The lords were led inside while the guard stabled the beasts and set a watch.

After the magi had settled into their chambers, Yochanan informed them that he had sent inquiries and gifts to his contacts at court to ask after an audience with the king. Melchior's cook offered assistance to the household chef, who was surprised and gratified to learn that the Parthian was familiar with preparing meals according to the Jewish ceremonial law—a skill he'd learned while hosting the Jewish scholars of Susa. The welcoming banquet was a grand success, all the more appreciated after weeks of camp cooking and inn fare.

Even as they were reclining at table, word came from Yochanan's contacts. Few things remained secret for long in Herod's Jerusalem, and the entrance parade of the magi had been noticed by many eyes. Their request for an audience had been granted, and the king would receive them the day after tomorrow.

This news, though welcome, nearly threw the household into a panic. Not even two days! Even those accustomed to the whims of the mercurial Herod were shocked. They'd been expecting at least a week, more likely two, to rest and prepare and get briefed on the latest court news. This barely gave them time to iron out the court robes!

The next day was a flurry of activity as servants scurried about making preparations. One of Yochanan's friends who frequented the court came to instruct them in the protocols Herod preferred. Though Gaspar was the youngest of their number, they chose him to be the main spokesman, since he'd had the most experience working with these sort of potentates. They found rich boxes for presenting the gifts they'd brought. Finally the busy day ended with a modest supper and the magi retiring with the realization that the morrow would bring them to the goal of their journey.

Their audience was for the fourth hour, but Tigranes was up before dawn to turn out and inspect the guard. Only a dozen spears were escorting the magi to Herod's palace, but with the wear and damage of the journey to deal with, it took almost that much time to get everyone and their gear squared away. Tigranes himself was just putting the final touches on his own boots when the lords came out to mount their steeds for the trip through the city.

"They look quite exotic," commented Yochanan, who was standing at the door near Tigranes.

"They're accustomed to court visits," Tigranes replied, not adding that the standards of the Parthian emperor's court in Seleucia were much higher than those of Herod's court in Jerusalem.

"Not to pry into my guests' personal concerns," Yochanan said in a wheedling voice, "but is there a reason for my lords' audience? Is it just a visit of state? Do they seek a treaty of some nature?"

"Oh, it's no secret," Tigranes said, surprised the topic hadn't been discussed. He supposed it had been lost in all the bustle. "They're here to congratulate the king on the birth of his son the prince."

"His—son?" Yochanan was looking puzzled and wary.

"Yes," Tigranes continued as he tightened a girth. "We realize we're several months late, but –"

"Captain," Yochanan interrupted sharply, now looking frightened. "There has been no prince born. All the king's sons who have survived are grown men."

"No prince?" Tigranes asked, puzzled in turn. "But the –"

"Captain, your lords cannot go before Herod speaking of a new prince!" Yochanan grabbed Tigranes' arm fiercely. "You have no idea how Herod –"

But just then the herald who had arrived to escort them to the palace rapped his staff on the ground, indicating that it was time to depart for the audience. Tigranes was the only one not yet on his horse, and his place was at the head of the small column of guards. He mounted with a concerned glance at Yochanan, who appeared terrified. Were they walking into a diplomatic catastrophe? Should they have researched the matter more carefully before marching into the king's presence? Too late to do anything about it now—the order of the parade had been dictated by the protocol officers, and any variation from it would draw notice and suspicion. Perhaps he'd have a chance to pull Gaspar aside before they were admitted to the throne room. But for now Tigranes had to ride in his prescribed place, just behind the herald. Behind him were his men with shined buckles jingling, and behind them were the lords in their court finery, and behind them came the horses laden with boxes of gifts. The crier who walked ahead of the herald cleared the streets for their passage.

When the party arrived at the palace gates, Tigranes and the guard were escorted aside while a flurry of courtiers greeted the magi. Sending his horse to the stable with another guard, Tigranes sought to get close to the lords, but it was impossible. He attached himself to the crowd, hoping that they'd be escorted to a waiting area where he could speak with the magi before the audience began, but it was a vain hope. Apparently things in Jerusalem were rather slow just then, for there were no other petitioners before them. They were escorted straight into the throne room, where the magi were placed in the center of the room while everyone else lined the edges. Tigranes tried to edge within whispering distance of Gaspar, but the lords' attention was being monopolized by some officious courtier, probably the palace steward. Herod had not yet arrived, so Tigranes continued to work his way toward the magi. He had almost made it when there was a blare of horns and rumble of drums. All knelt and bowed as the steward announced the king's entrance. There was the sound of jingling and huffing as Herod ascended his throne.

Then the command was given to rise, and Tigranes got his first glimpse of Herod the Great.

Herod was a squat man, rotund like many kings who grow in the love of the table as they get older. He wore his hair and beard long in the Jewish style, and his neck was adorned with thick gold chains while his fingers were heavy with rings. In his face Tigranes could see a trace of the decisiveness that had earned him his title, but it had long since faded beneath the flab and wrinkles that had overtaken him. Herod's dark eyes glittered as he surveyed the room, and Tigranes could not decide whether it was with intelligence or malice—or both.

Tigranes noticed that behind the throne, a little to Herod's right, stood a thin man with dark, heavily lidded eyes. The man was not wearing the gaudy clothes that the other courtiers were, but rather a sparse, trimly cut tunic that looked like a uniform. In his belt he wore a long dagger and his eyes scanned the room warily. He had not been present before, so Tigranes presumed he'd arrived with the king. Tigranes was almost certain who this man was—he'd seen the type many times before. This was Herod's hatchet man, his personal assassin, the one assigned the dirty jobs. The man eyed the magi carefully then looked to where Tigranes stood. Observing his livery and proximity to the visitors, the man caught Tigranes' eyes and nodded slowly, as if acknowledging a colleague. Tigranes nodded in return, but wasn't sure if he wanted to be thought any kind of comrade of this man.

Now the court formalities were being followed, with the steward introducing the magi and Gaspar stepping up to do the talking. After the usual flowery words the gifts were brought forward. Tigranes had known about the gifts, since keeping them secure had been one of his highest priorities, but this was the first time he'd seen them. They were princely—bolts of fine silk and caskets of rare spices and finely wrought Persian metalware and a set of exquisite porcelain which Tigranes was sure they hadn't had before staying at the house of Shamshi-Adad in Hatra. These gifts set a good tone for the main thrust of the audience.

"We receive your gifts," Herod rumbled in a gravelly voice. "Pray, tell us what is your embassy to our court? What brings such esteemed personages to our door?"

Tigranes tensed. If Yochanan was right, this was where things could get anything from embarrassing to dangerous, depending on how Herod responded. But Tigranes could hardly jump out and interrupt, so Gaspar just continued as they'd planned, unaware of what he was walking into.

"Most glorious majesty, whose countenance illuminates the earth, we seek no boon or profit from your gracious hand," Gaspar intoned formally. "We have come only to do honor to the newborn heir, king of the Jews, whose coming was written in the skies and foretold in the ancient scriptures."

The throne room fell dead silent. Nobody dared move or speak or, seemingly, breathe. Herod's robes rustled as he resettled himself on his throne.

"My...heir?" the king asked in a throaty whisper.

"Yes, your gracious majesty," Gaspar continued, seemingly oblivious to the tension crackling in the air. "Upon observing such great signs in the eastern skies, and above Jerusalem, we undertook to study the writings of the great prophets and seers of your people. We found foretold the coming of the mighty son of David, and the inauguration of his great reign. In deference to him whom even the heavens salute, we have come here to honor him—and, of course, his exulted father."

"The son of David?" Herod asked, barely audible this time.

"Yes, your illustrious majesty," Gaspar replied. "But perhaps I should defer to our master, who is much more learned in these matters." They had anticipated having Melchior doing the more technical explanations, which he proceeded to do, leaning more on the prophetic writings than on the astrological phenomena, given the audience. He spoke of the visions of Dani'el and their interpretations, and how accurate they'd been regarding other kingdoms, and the count of years, and the witness of the skies. He explained how all these factors together had drawn them to David's ancient city to do homage to David's heir.

Through all this explaining, Tigranes could see that Melchior was also unaware of the atmosphere in the throne room, though it seemed like Gaspar and Balthazar were starting to catch on. The courtiers were glancing at each other nervously, looking like they'd rather be anywhere else. Herod glowered down at the magi while the dark-eyed man behind the throne gazed at them with sinister fascination.

At last Melchior finished, and again the room was deathly quiet.

"The son of David?" Herod asked, then pushed himself to his feet. "The son of David? The line of David has been wiped out, do you hear? Extinguished, centuries ago! There is no line of David, except in the legends and dreams of fools!" His voice was rising now, and he was brandishing his scepter at the magi.

"But...the ancient writings..." stammered Melchior in confusion.

"The ancient writings! The ancient writings!" Herod cried, throwing up his hands in mock alarm. "For a drachma you can find a scholar who will interpret the ancient writings any way you wish. The line of David is dead. I am the king of the Jews, and my line will rule for a thousand years! Ancient writings! Signs in the skies! Fools! Leave my court! I have no patience for mumbling mages and chattering seers!" With that he stormed out in a rustle of fabric, his henchman close on his heels.

The throne room emptied quickly. Courtiers who had come to savor the cachet of the exotic visitors suddenly remembered urgent business elsewhere, so there was a clamor for the exits. Soon the magi and Tigranes were all that remained, along with a minor court official to whom the steward had assigned the task of showing the now unwelcome foreigners to the door.

"My lords, I am deeply sorry," Tigranes said. "I was warned by Yochanan just as we were leaving that matters might not stand as we thought they did, but I had no chance to warn you."

"Nobody blames you, Tigranes," Gaspar assured him. "Come, let us return to the house," He and Balthazar took Melchior's elbows and led him toward the door. Tigranes took the lead, just behind the courtier, to get back to the guard and other servants and tell them to saddle up. This was done in short order, and the company headed away from the palace with much less fanfare than they'd had going to it. Melchior was still looking stunned and confused, and Tigranes watched him closely as they rode.

They had not gone half a mile when they heard some cries from behind, and running feet. Tigranes fell back to see a messenger overtaking them. Even though the runner wore palace livery, Tigranes dropped his spear across the way to halt him.

"Here, now, what do you want?" Tigranes asked gruffly.

"The...the king's steward requests the eastern lords return to the palace," the man panted.

"The steward? For what purpose?" Tigranes asked.

"For consultation. That was all he said."

Tigranes glanced at Gaspar, who had ridden back to join him. A return summons after an audience that had gone so badly was not encouraging, but they could hardly ignore it. There was also the question of how to return. Should the entire company go? Just the magi?

Gaspar solved this dilemma for Tigranes. "We will return. Gordias, Tetius, accompany us. Tigranes, send the rest home and come with us—but warn them not to disarm or unsaddle." This last was said in a low voice inaudible to the messenger. Shortly thereafter the six men were riding back through the palace gates, where a servant showed them into a side chamber. When the servant tried to close the door after the magi had entered, Gaspar blocked him and held it open until the three guards had followed.

The palace steward was in the room, pacing nervously. At the lords' arrival he bid them be seated at a table on which he had placed a pitcher of wine and four goblets. With a forced smile the steward himself filled the goblets, though he did not sit down. Tigranes and the other guards took their places along the walls.

"I thank you for returning so promptly, especially after such a—after that audience," the steward stammered, bobbing his head as he paced. "His majesty has instructed me to assure you that he appreciates your gifts, and I'm sure—that is, he has had many concerns of late, and was not feeling his best this morning, and—and I'm sure he regrets his abruptness toward the end."

The magi looked at one another. This was certainly the closest they were going to get to a royal apology, but it still left the question of what they were doing here.

"The king's grace is too kind," Balthazar said noncommittally.

"Without straining my lords' patience, the king has one more request which he hopes you can accommodate."

"Which is?" Gaspar asked.

"The king would like his horoscope cast. It is not often that astrologers of such repute make it to Jerusalem, and he was hoping…that is, he did not want to pass up the opportunity."

Again the lords looked at each other. "Not often" was a mild way of putting it. Due to Jewish religious sensibilities, astrologers weren't even tolerated in Judea, much less Jerusalem. But given that, what would a Jewish king want with a horoscope?

Melchior, as the preeminent astrologer of the group, did not answer, but sat looking at his untouched wine goblet. Balthazar finally spoke up.

"Please inform the king that we will be happy to cast his horoscope. We will need certain personal details about his life, but will send a servant around for them in time."

"Thank you, thank you," the steward said with relief, bowing repeatedly.

"Is that all the king wished?" Gaspar asked.

"Yes, my lords," the steward assured him, bowing again. The magi rose and filed from the room, led by Gordias and Tetius and followed by Tigranes, who wanted to stay on foot until the others were safely on their horses. As he hung back by the door, scanning the courtyard while the others mounted, a smooth voice spoke from behind him.

"Captain—Tigranes, is it?"

Tigranes turned to see the dark-eyed man who'd been standing behind Herod's throne.

"May I ask who wishes to know?"

"Permit me," the man said with a slight bow. "I am Hadad, advisor to the king on matters of security and captain of his personal guard."

"Very well, Captain," Tigranes replied, returning the bow. "I am indeed Tigranes, servant of Lord Melchior. How may I be of service?"

"I do not wish to delay you now," Hadad waved at the others. "But I was wondering if, sometime during your visit, you would wish to accompany me on my rounds about the city? I thought someone with common interest and background might find the experience illuminating."

Tigranes looked at the man's eyes and partially lifted eyebrow. *In other words, Captain, you've been assigned to milk me for information, and I know you've been so assigned, and you presume that I'd know that you've been assigned, but we're just supposed to casually chat as if none of this was going on?* But what he said was, "Of course, Captain. Feel free to call at your convenience."

They nodded and Tigranes mounted and rode after the others, who were already filing out of the palace gates.

Back at Yochanan's house, their host was awaiting them anxiously. Word of the debacle in the throne room had reached him even before the first guard had returned. Wringing his hands and looking pale, he escorted the magi to a sitting room where wine and cakes awaited.

"My lords, I am so terribly sorry," Yochanan said, bowing repeatedly. "I should have inquired into your intentions before letting you go off to Herod's palace. And when I heard you had been summoned back, I feared the worst –"

"None of this is your fault, friend," Balthazar assured him. "We should have asked our own questions before accepting an audience with the king clothed in nothing more than our own assumptions. Let us ask these questions now: from the king's response, I presume he is not of the line of David, and has no recent issue?"

"The line of David?" A startled Yochanan replied, as if someone had just walked across his grave. "No, my lords. Herod is not even Jewish."

"But—isn't he king, *ethnarch*, of the Jews?" Gaspar asked.

"Rome says he is, but he's actually of Idumea, an ancient nation to our south, distantly related to us. They are known in our history as Edom," Yochanan explained. "Though as with the people of Samaria to the north, there has been much intermingling over the centuries, and few anymore can claim pure Jewish—or Edomite—blood. Also, about a century ago, during the Hasmonean reign, Jerusalem claimed jurisdiction over Idumea, and forced their people to accept Judaism."

"So that's the foundation of Herod's claim to the Jewish throne?" Balthazar asked.

"He also married Miryam, or Mariamne in the Greek form, to strengthen his claim."

"Was she of the line of David?" Melchior asked weakly.

"No, my lord," Yochanan said. "A daughter of the Hasmoneans, she was of the line of Levi."

"And I guarantee you the Romans care nothing for such dynastic nuances," Gaspar added. "They want a strong ruler who can maintain order and keep the revenues flowing. If they get one who even smells Jewish, that will be good enough for them."

"Herod tries harder than that," Yochanan said. "He claims to follow the Law, and recognizes the authority of the high priest. But he is terribly jealous of his throne, to the point of killing his own wife and sons to protect it. He would not welcome news of a child born of any other line, particularly the line of David."

Melchior reclined at the table, his wine untouched, his bread broken but barely tasted, staring vacantly at nothing. "So," he said in a voice just barely above a whisper. "The son of David is not seated in Jerusalem, and a foreigner holds the throne."

"Not exactly a foreigner…" began Yochanan, glancing about nervously as if worried they might be overheard.

"Bel'Tshazzar was wrong," Melchior continued in a hollow voice.

"Who was wrong?" Yochanan asked.

"I beg your pardon," Melchior said suddenly. "I—I must retire." He rose from the table and wandered away. Gaspar and Balthazar watched gravely as he departed.

Before retiring that evening, Yochanan sought out Balthazar and Gaspar. Melchior had remained in his chambers all day, not even coming out for the evening meal.

"My sources tell me that the king summoned the leading priests and temple scholars to his palace this afternoon. The question posed to them was where the long-foretold son of David would be born."

"What did they say?" Balthazar asked.

"Beit-Lechem," Yochanan answered.

"Beit-Lechem?"

"It's a small farming village not far from here," Yochanan explained. "The ancient birthplace of the great king David, a thousand years ago."

"Hmm—sounds more like folklore," Balthazar mused.

"It's what the prophet said," Yochanan replied.

"Did the king indicate whether he was going to do anything?"

"My sources didn't say, but then, you can rarely tell when Herod's going to do something."

"We'll have to see what tomorrow brings," Balthazar said.

One thing it brought, right after the morning meal, was a visitor: Hadad, inviting Tigranes to accompany him on an early patrol of the city. Tigranes had discussed Hadad's offer, and his certain true purpose, with Balthazar and Gaspar, and they had encouraged him to provide the king's officer with any information he wished. Everything about their journey was open and above-board, which didn't mean someone might not read some nefarious intent into it, but there was no reason to raise unnecessary suspicions.

Tigranes and Hadad were exquisitely cordial to one another, partly to veil their mutual dislike. Tigranes bridled at Hadad's superior manner, and sensed the captain knew of and relished this. Tigranes figured someone in Hadad's position had to at least tolerate being detested, but he tried to keep his answers brisk and businesslike. They walked through the streets and along the walls of Jerusalem in no order that Tigranes could discern, and what guards they met did not respond to Hadad as if he was any kind of watch officer. Feigning merely casual interest, Hadad asked many questions about the magi: where they had come from, why they had come, what their sources of information were. He seemed particularly interested in Gaspar's martial experience and Balthazar's recent travels through the region. Tigranes couldn't give much detail there, but told what he could.

For his part, Tigranes kept his return questions simple and innocuous, not wishing to give the impression that he was prying for information about the court. He found it interesting that Hadad spent almost no time discussing the temple, which was not only the most imposing edifice in Jerusalem but his master's signature achievement. Tigranes wondered if being stationed in the city had caused Hadad to grow blasé about the temple. He shortly learned in a most brutal and shocking manner that there was more to Hadad's disdain.

The morning was getting warm, and they were walking in some of the narrower streets in a poorer section of the city. It did not escape Tigranes' notice that people seemed to know Hadad by sight, as evidenced by the way they ducked into doorways or down side streets when they spotted him coming. But there was one unfortunate exception: an older woman who was pottering about in front of a house. When Hadad came into view she initially froze, then cried out and started toward him, her arms waving vigorously.

"My husband! What have you done with him? It has been over two months now! Where have you taken him? Bring him back!" The woman seemed oblivious to her danger, and started flailing at Hadad with futile blows. He caught one of her wrists and began beating the woman brutally with his fist.

Just then a young man came to the door of the house. "Mother!" he cried, dashing for her, his face contorted with rage. Hadad's blows had knocked the woman to the pavement, and she was trying to shield herself with her one free arm. Then the lad stepped in, trying to catch Hadad's arm and pull her out of his grip.

It all happened so quickly that Tigranes didn't even see it. Suddenly the lad was stumbling and gasping, Hadad's dagger buried in his chest to the hilt. With an expression of brutal satisfaction, Hadad yanked the knife out, and the boy collapsed onto his mother, drenching her in blood.

"Come, Captain," Hadad said, turning and walking away as if nothing had happened while the woman began screaming in shock and horror. Tigranes stood stunned, staring at the boy's quivering body and the now hysterical woman. Every instinct urged him to help, but it was clear that nothing could be done for the boy, and faces were starting to look out of doorways—faces wearing harsh and hostile expressions. Tigranes realized that even though he was a Jew, he was still a stranger and a foreigner, and any protection that Hadad's office provided would not extend to him if he were to be caught alone. Shaking in horror, he followed Hadad as people began to converge on the tragic scene.

"My apologies that you had to witness that regrettable incident of rebellion," Hadad said briskly as he wiped his dagger clean with a kerchief. "Perhaps it is time for another civil order campaign."

"Did that woman...her husband..." Tigranes stammered.

"I don't know," Hadad replied. "I think that he was picked up in connection with some subversive group. It's impossible to keep track of them all."

"But...her son?"

"One fewer of them, so far as I'm concerned," Hadad said with a shrug. "Impossible people. Someone should do mankind a favor and wipe them off the face of the earth."

Tigranes looked at him in surprise. "But—aren't they your people?"

Hadad gave Tigranes a look of scorn laced with disgust. "*My* people? Please, Captain. I'm no Jew. I come from the same race as the king—the ancient tribe of Edom, firstborn son and true heir. These Jews are descended from Ya'kov the Grasper, a liar, cheat, and thief, and they all follow in his footsteps. In fact, my family is of the clan of Amelek, who were the first of my people to recognize the threat these Jews posed."

Tigranes was feeling lightheaded and nauseated, and his hands were still trembling in shock. "I…ah…should we summon someone about…?" He gestured back toward the murdered boy. "A trivial matter—they'll deal with it," Hadad said, waving dismissively. "But the sun does grow warm. Perhaps we should return to your house."

Back at the house, Tigranes mentioned nothing to anyone of what had happened, but began to think that the sooner they were away from Jerusalem, with its volatile ruler and his brutal minions, the better.

That night was clear, so Balthazar and Gaspar were up on the roof, taking the initial sightings for the horoscope they'd promised for the king. Melchior would have been the best person for this, but there was no getting him out of his room for any reason. The two friends spoke in low, concerned tones about their master's condition. Since the shock of learning of the state of affairs in Jerusalem, Melchior had sunk into an even greater despondency than he'd been in when they'd arrived at his estate over a year before. Then he'd been nearly at the point of despair, but the seeming convergence of the signs in the skies and the ancient Jewish writings had revitalized him, giving him hope and purpose. The discovery that the ancient writings had been wrong, that the king in Jerusalem wasn't of David's line and had no newborn son, had crushed the old man.

"And there hangs Jupiter in the southern sky," Gaspar pointed. "It's all his fault, you know. That triple-conjunction with Regulus, then the conjunction with Venus. We believed you, old boy! Why did you let us down?"

The days passed slowly, filled with gloomy tension. Melchior eventually recovered some equilibrium, but settled into a grim fatalism that wasn't typical of him. For their part, the two other magi realized that they weren't sure what was next for them, either. They'd been swept along on this journey by Melchior's vision and enthusiasm, assuming that whatever they found at the end would fundamentally change something for them. Now that the journey had proven to be based on an error and had come to nothing, they weren't sure what came next. When Gaspar had showed up at Melchior's gate, he'd been at loose ends, and had been contemplating continuing on to his homeland. That prospect now seemed flat and insipid, and a grueling journey as well. He'd traveled a thousand miles in the wrong direction, back to the edge of the Roman world. Well, perhaps he'd try his luck with the Romans again, or find some king who could use his services. Or maybe being general of Alwenah wouldn't be so bad after all, if the job was still open.

Balthazar also struggled, but his doubts were deeper and darker. He had discussed the import of Bel'Tshazzar's visions with the Persian and Jewish scholars, and had grasped what lay behind them: pure religion. The visions were about far more than the fate of this or that earthly kingdom, and which king would reign next. It was about right knowledge, and pure worship, of the True God. That was what Bel'Tshazzar's mysterious 'son of man' was—the Rock uncut by human hands. Since the dawn of civilization men had been building towers and idols, ostensibly to honor their gods, but actually to exult and aggrandize themselves. That had been the meaning of the statue of gold and silver and bronze and iron in the Babylonian emperor's dream— a symbolic composite of all the idols of man, formed by his own hands for him to bow down before. Balthazar had known from the moment he'd heard it the symbolism of the Rock uncut by human hands, the Rock that smashed the statue then swelled to fill the entire earth. The Jewish god—*the* God, if their writings were to be believed—was tired of the towers of men, and would establish His own tower. That, Balthazar realized, was what he'd come seeking.

But now it all seemed for naught. The towers of Herod's temple reached as high as any other towers, and for the same reason. The Jewish priesthood seemed as petty and self-absorbed as any priestly caste Balthazar had seen in his travels. He now wondered if all his searching and hoping and lofty idealism was merely dust. Maybe there was no pure worship. Maybe there was nothing more than the towers of men, crowding the skies, the new ones built on the ruins of the old, all managed by endless generations of fussy priests with their rules and rituals. Maybe it was his fate to live out his days as one of them—maybe even at the altar of Atargatis.

The status of the magi in Jerusalem was uncertain. They'd committed to casting Herod's horoscope, which would call for periodic sky sightings across the span of about two weeks. Once that was done, they weren't certain what came next. The king had not dismissed them, but they had, in a way, accomplished what they'd come for. They'd obtained their audience and presented their gifts. There should be no reason they couldn't just take their leave once they'd completed the horoscope—except that Herod wasn't a man you took chances with.

One evening Gaspar and Balthazar were up on the roof for the last of their sky sightings. They both had their notes and records of the positions and angles of various stars, and were taking the final sights before assembling the document to deliver to Herod.

"Well," Gaspar said lightly, jotting something on a page. "If I interpret these signs aright, the king won't live another year."

"Don't include that," Balthazar chuckled.

"But his line will endure," Gaspar examined his notes. "Though the Water-Bearer—Aquarius as the Greeks call him—figures largely in their future. Make of that what you will."

Balthazar was busy getting a star angle. With a puzzled look he glanced back through his notes, then took the angle again.

"Gaspar," he asked. "What do you have for an angle of Jupiter to Alpha Pegasi?"

"Let me see," Gaspar mused, flipping through some pages then looking at Balthazar's notes in mystification. "We couldn't have both gotten it wrong."

"And here's tonight's angle," Balthazar tapped a figure. Gaspar gazed at the number, muttering, then looked slowly up at his friend.

"The angle is supposed to be increasing, but it isn't. Jupiter has stopped."

"He's not just stopped," Balthazar added. "He's going backward. He's in retrograde."

While Gaspar pondered this, Balthazar ran to the stairway and called for their host. In a minute he stood beside them, looking worried.

"Yochanan," Balthazar asked. "This Beit-Lechem—in which direction does it lie?"

"Beit-Lechem, my lord? Due south, about five miles. On a clear day you can see it from certain parts of Jerusalem."

South. Gaspar and Balthazar looked at each other with wide eyes.

"Get Melchior," Balthazar ordered.

THE ROAD SOUTH

"Yes, no question," Melchior said half an hour later, peering at the figures. "Jupiter has stopped, and is going backwards in his course." The old man's voice was weak, and in the dim lamplight that illuminated the shelter on the corner of the roof he looked even worse than he did in daylight. His skin was pale and stretched and his eyes were hollow. Balthazar had seen the look before: a man for whom life was empty of meaning, a man who had lost his inner purpose, a man close to giving up.

"And south of us! Due south, right over Beit-Lechem!" Gaspar said with excitement, pointing across the darkened hills.

"Yes," Melchior sighed wearily. "But this is Jupiter, who has lied to us before."

"Has he?" Balthazar asked sharply. He'd been pondering that very question as he'd paced the rooftop awaiting Melchior's arrival. "Has he? Since we saw the signs in the heavens and read the sacred writings, we've been looking for the son of David. *We* were the ones who made the assumption that he would be found in Jerusalem. But thinking back, I can't remember any of the scholars saying that. They said he would *rule* from Jerusalem, not that he would be born there. The temple scholars told Herod without hesitation that the child would be born in Beit-Lechem."

"But Jerusalem is where the king is! And there is no child!" Melchior answered.

"We wouldn't expect a child here, because Herod is of the wrong line," Balthazar explained. "Rome enthroned Herod over this region for their own purposes. He's a rock cut by human hands. From the perspective of the dream Bel'Tshazzar interpreted, he's not even in the picture, except perhaps as one of those clay toes that gets smashed. The line of Herod means nothing—it's the line of David that matters."

"The line of David! The line of David!" cried Melchior in exasperation, throwing up his hands. "There is no line of David! It was cut off generations ago!"

"So says Herod," Balthazar challenged him. "So say the priests running the temple establishment who are so cozy with Herod and the Romans. But the sacred writings say differently, and so," he jabbed his finger in the direction of Jupiter, "does the sky above."

Melchior sighed and collapsed into a chair, muttering.

"There's one thing nobody has yet done," Gaspar added from where he sat on the low wall that ran about the roof edge. "For all the prophesies and star gazing and discussion, nobody's actually done the obvious thing."

"Go to Beit-Lechem," Balthazar said quietly.

Melchior sighed and bowed his head. "What if we get there and find nothing? After all this disappointment –"

"What disappointment?" Gaspar asked, leaping to his feet. "What have we learned here? That Herod isn't of David's line? We knew that. That he has no newborn son? It wouldn't matter if he had. That the line of David is extinguished? As Balthazar points out, the experts say that, but the ancient writings and the skies say otherwise."

"But the star stood over Jerusalem!" Melchior protested.

"The star stood in the west," Balthazar replied. "From where we were in Persia, it was as much over Beit-Lechem as Jerusalem. So we came west to Jerusalem, and now that we're here, the star stands south over Beit-Lechem."

"The very place the Jewish seers say the child would be born," Gaspar added. "Listen, master—we traveled a thousand miles because the skies and ancient writings agreed. Now they're agreeing again, and we only have to go five more miles to ascertain the truth of the matter. Let's not falter just as the champion's wreath draws into view."

"But what if there's nothing there?" Melchior repeated.

"Then we'll be proven fools who traveled a thousand and five miles to no purpose, because of our vanity and wishful thinking," Balthazar replied. "But I like Gaspar's point—what if we traveled a thousand miles only to give up and not realize our goal because we were unwilling to go five more miles? Which would be the greater folly?"

Melchior's head drooped, and he sat hunched over, shaking his head. "My friends, I cannot. Leave me here, and go on without me."

"Leave you here?" Balthazar asked. "Master, this was your idea from the beginning! It would not be right for you to not be there at the end."

"I am too worn down. I could not bear another disappointment. I simply lack the strength," Melchior sighed.

"I once knew a lad," Gaspar chimed in. "Who was exasperated by his schoolwork. He was far from home, struggling in a strange land, frustrated by the new languages, and taxed by the severe curriculum. He suffered more setbacks and disappointments than he thought he could bear, and was ready to give up. His schoolmaster found him in the garden one day, in tears and close to despair, ready to quit the school and take a boat back to his home. The master encouraged him to stay a little longer, to try a little harder, that relief from the worst of his trials was just around the corner. In short, he encouraged the lad to hope. And you know what? The schoolmaster was right. Within a few weeks the lad was finding his footing in his studies, and before long he was doing as well as all the other students. He ended up being a very successful student at that school, all because he'd taken his master's advice and tried just a little harder."

Melchior sat silent for a minute, nodding slightly. Then he slowly lifted his head and looked at his friends with a ghost of a smile and a hint of a familiar light in his eyes.

"Very well. Let us go to Beit-Lechem. If we're to be fools, let's be great fools! Let us go the final five miles and be proven in our folly, or…or…"

"Or find the son of David," Gaspar completed quietly.

The question of their uncertain status remained, but now that they had a goal, they decided to push the matter. After all, the king had given them no instructions, and had requested nothing of them but the horoscope. They decided to finish writing that up the next day and present it at the palace—no need for another audience—and then quietly but publicly leave the city the following day.

As they were attending to this plan the next morning, they got an unsettling interruption in the form of a messenger who claimed to be from the palace, requesting the magi attend a private audience with the king later that day. The man did not look like a herald, and wore no palace livery, but they did not doubt that he came from the king. In Jerusalem, nobody claimed to be speaking in Herod's name unless they were. The magi discussed this request among themselves, wondering if their rooftop conversation might have been overheard. But in the end they had to agree, there being no other option. The messenger told them he would return at the proper time to guide them, which mystified them further—they knew the way to the palace. They grew even more concerned when the messenger stipulated that it had to be only the magi—no guards or aides would be allowed. But Gaspar reasoned that the king was probably not planning any skullduggery, since he could simply send a squad of guards at any time to do whatever he wished to them. But that did not comfort them much when the messenger returned in the early afternoon—again, not wearing palace livery—to lead them through the narrow streets of Jerusalem.

Baba had enjoyed the stay in Jerusalem. He'd learned enough on the journey to be able to discern that something was distressing the grownups, but all that meant was that they were attending to him less. Other than the minor tasks which the captain found for him, his time was his own, and he'd used it to explore the ancient and exotic city. He'd made friends with the housekeeper, who had two sons about his age who'd been happy to show him about the alleys and rooftops, and warn him out of the areas he should stay away from, not being a Jew. They'd spent long afternoons wandering Jerusalem, being sure to avoid watchful adult eyes. Before long, Baba felt confident of his knowledge of the city streets.

Which was why he decided to discreetly follow the magi that afternoon when the palace messenger came to escort the lords to the audience. Captain Tigranes was not at all happy that the king was insisting that they come without guards, and that nobody knew where they were going. The captain couldn't send men to follow them, because that would apparently be a grave insult to the king. There was nothing that could be done, and Tigranes was left to pace the courtyard and snap at the men in his anxiety. He took no notice of Baba, which was what gave Baba the idea: if the captain didn't notice him, who would? He slipped unheeded out of the gates and followed the messenger and the three lords at a cautious distance.

For their part, the magi were mystified and slightly concerned as they were led through the streets. They were not going toward the palace, and the messenger could say nothing about what the king wished of them. The messenger finally stopped in front of a house on a nondescript street and beckoned them through the door. It was a large house, not so large as

Yochanan's but bigger than most in the city. It had two stories, and the roof was edged with trellises thick with some type of vine.

They entered the house to find another servant who bid them follow him up the stairs, through the second floor, and to the stairs that led up to the roof. There was nobody on the second floor, and the servant simply beckoned for them to ascend, not going up the stairs himself.

On the rooftop they found the king seated at a table whereon were set some refreshments. There was nobody else present, not even the henchman whom Tigranes so loathed. Startled, the magi knelt, but the king bid them rise and join him at the table, where wine had already been poured. Up close, and without his court finery, Herod looked unwell—fat and dissipated, with yellow eyes and bad teeth, accompanied by a vague pestilential odor. Gaspar could well believe he wouldn't live out the year. But his glance retained the same animal cunning—he was yet dangerous.

"Your majesty," Gaspar began, drawing a scroll from his bag. "At your request, we have prepared for you this horoscope, based on the information you provided and our observations of the skies."

"Yes—ah—thank you," Herod said vaguely, taking the scroll and setting it aside. "My lords, I have summoned you here to ask about—ah—your journey. I wished to converse with you away from the palace, which has ears in the strangest places— you know about court intrigues."

The magi assured him that they did, and he proceeded to ask them many questions about the celestial events which had impelled their journey. Melchior answered most of these, this time stressing the astrological aspects of their research and downplaying what they'd learned from the Jewish scholars. Herod attended to it all, but seemed particularly interested in the timing.

"A year ago this past September," he asked several times. "That's when you saw the first of these heavenly signs?"

They assured him of this, until he finally seemed satisfied. Then he startled them all with a request they hadn't anticipated.

"We have consulted with our scholars and court officials," Herod rumbled. "And we have concluded that we acted a bit— ah—hastily in dismissing the idea that an heir of David's line may have been born. It seems unlikely, but with such portents in the heavens, and a journey by such noble lords as yourselves, we have been reconsidering whether there might be something to all this. Of course, to us—ah—Jews, the prospect of a son of David's line is a matter of the greatest excitement, no less for me than for the least—ah—shepherd. Given the promises, if such a birth were to occur, it would be a most welcome development. If, of course, there is any such birth. With a populace as volatile and excitable as mine, one does not wish to encourage rumors and speculations, so a direct investigation by myself would be— ah—difficult.

"Thus we were wondering if you noble lords would be willing to assist us in this matter. We would not want such an opportunity as the birth of the heir of David to—well, it would have great significance for me and all my people. Would you be willing to discreetly search out this matter for us? To determine if there is anything to all this? For if the long-promised son of David has been born, we would wish—that is, we would like to come do him honor as well."

"We would be happy to serve the king in any way we could," Gaspar answered carefully.

"Good, good," Herod replied. "I knew you would be helpful. My scholars tell me that the place where the foretold child would be born is Beit-Lechem, a little town just south of here. Any local can direct you there. If you find anything, please return with news as quickly as possible. But my lords, if you please—keep this mission secret."

* * *

It had been a simple matter for Baba to shadow the magi to their destination. Once he was at the house, working his way around to the far wall and climbing up to the second floor proved a bit more challenging. But there were enough handholds and protruding beam ends in the wall for him to scramble up quietly. Well hidden from the street and barely daring to breathe, he stuck his head up over the edge of the wall around the rooftop. The vines were thick here, so he had to part the leaves a bit to see through them. He was used to seeing the lords, but this would be his first chance to see the king that everyone in Jerusalem was so afraid of!

To Baba's amazement, there were only the lords and the king on the rooftop—no courtiers, no court dress, not even any guards. Baba was sure this was unusual, given what he'd heard of kings, but he didn't know what it meant. He kept as still as a mouse—fortunately his footing was solidly placed on a beam end—and listened. His perch was barely ten feet from the table at which the lords were sitting, so he could hear much of what they were saying despite the leaves.

They were mostly talking about dull grown-up stuff, though Baba did hear them mention Beit-Lechem, which was where they were supposed to be going tomorrow. Had the king known about that? Wasn't it a big secret? Baba wasn't impressed by the king. He'd seen two kings on this journey. The king of Alwenah hadn't looked like much, but Baba had thought that was because Alwenah was such a small, out-of-the-way city, little more than a village. But this was the king of Jerusalem, an old and famous city. This king had been to Rome and ruled a large territory, but he looked like any other pudgy old man, and he coughed a lot. He wasn't even wearing a crown! But the lords answered him respectfully.

Now the lords were standing up, though the king remained seated. They bowed to him and backed away toward the door.

They seemed to have agreed to do something for him. Once they had left, the king remained seated. Baba watched him for a while, just because he could, and out of curiosity over what he would do. The king sat while the sound of the lords mounting up and riding away came from the street below. Baba had just concluded that he'd seen all there was to see, and was preparing to climb down, when a thin man came through the door onto the rooftop patio. Baba didn't like the man, who looked mean.

"You will have them trailed, of course," the king said to the man.

"I will attend to it myself, your majesty," the man replied. "I'll select my most experienced men."

"Kill everyone they speak with in Beit-Lechem," the king instructed. "Just to be certain."

"And they themselves?" the man asked.

"Them, of course, and any immediate attendants," the king replied. "Preferably without involving their entire company— I'd like you back."

"Please, sire," the man replied with a dismissive wave. "I know how to deal with caravan guards."

"Very well—I leave matters to your judgment."

"Thank you, your majesty," the man said with a bow, then departed.

Baba held his breath, his heart hammering. He knew enough to understand what all that meant! He had to get back and tell someone! But who? Not Lord Gaspar—he'd be furious when he learned that Baba had been spying on him. Captain Tigranes would know what to do, though he would certainly scold him for being so naughty.

"You did *what*?" Captain Tigranes nearly shouted, grabbing Baba by the shoulders and shaking him. "Baba, do you realize— had you been caught, you would have been killed! Immediately, without mercy, and with no consideration of your youth! None of us could have done a thing to help you!"

Baba could tell the captain was more than just angry. He was pale in a way that Baba had never seen, and his hands were trembling. Baba realized that the captain was frightened—badly frightened. Well, so was Baba, but he needed to tell the captain what he knew.

"I know, sir, but after the lords left, I heard the king talking to a man—a dark man."

"A dark man?" the captain asked sharply. "Did you hear his name?"

"No, sir, he didn't mention it. He and the king seemed to know each other. He was thin."

"I think I know who you're talking about," the captain said, starting to pace the floor. "What did they say to one another?"

Baba told him, shaking with fright at the retelling. The captain was focusing on him, though his hands were still trembling, and he asked Baba many questions.

"This is bad, isn't it, sir?" Baba asked when he'd finished.

"It's very bad, Baba," the captain replied. "And though what you did was very dangerous, I'm glad you came and told me what you'd heard."

"Would you like me to fetch Lord Gaspar, sir?"

The captain was silent for a minute, as if making up his mind. "No," he said at last. "Let's leave Gaspar out of this. Here's what you can do: you know Lord Gaspar's guards, Gordias and Tetius? Can you find them and ask them to come see me? Very quietly?"

"Yes, sir."

"And Baba—don't tell anyone what you've told me. Not Gordias and Tetius, not the lords, not the cook, not anyone, do you understand?"

"Yes, sir."

* * *

The next morning the magi and their caravan were at the western gate of Jerusalem as the sun was breaking the horizon. This was a change—they'd planned to take a leisurely morning packing and taking their leave of Yochanan. But Tigranes, citing unspecified "security concerns", had begged and pleaded and cajoled until they'd agreed to a crack of dawn departure. Gaspar, who deeply respected the Captain's judgment, had subtly pried regarding the nature of these concerns, but Tigranes had been tight-lipped, so Gaspar had let the matter rest. Gaspar wondered if it had anything to do with the mission Tigranes had sent Gordias and Tetius galloping off on the prior afternoon. They hadn't spoken much of that, either, though Gaspar gathered they'd been reconnoitering the south road the caravan would be taking this morning.

The early departure meant the company had been up hours before dawn, packing and saddling by torchlight. The whining and grumbling hadn't troubled Tigranes, who'd stalked about barking orders and goading people to hurry. He seemed to take extra care talking to the guard. Gaspar was starting to wonder if he shouldn't press the Captain a little harder for details on those security concerns.

The caravan was stretched out along the road, riding up and down the hills. A few of the guards were staying close to the lords, but most were scattered along the length of the caravan. Tigranes didn't expect to be troubled along this stretch of road.

In fact, this morning, along this stretch, he planned to be the one causing the trouble.

Tigranes was riding toward the back of the caravan with Gordias and Tetius beside him. They were going slowly, unobtrusively dropping back through the ranks until they were in the very rear.

"Do you think we gave them the slip by departing so early?" Gordias asked.

"Not Herod's men," Tigranes said. "They'd have been watching the house. The best we can hope for is to rattle them, surprise them into doing something hasty—which we'll be waiting for."

"Aye, Captain," Tetius said with a wicked grin. "The spot is just up ahead, beyond this rise. The leading guards should be passing it about now."

When the three topped the rise, they could see the caravan well along on the road ahead, and no sound of pursuit from behind—yet. Fortunately, the road was still empty of other traffic.

"Here it is, cap'n," Tetius pointed to a ridge that rose on the west side of the road, commanding a clear view of the hundred or so yards back to where the road dropped over the rise. Behind the ridge was a ravine thick with rocks, scrub, fallen logs, and other clutter.

"Tetius, Gordias, this is perfect," Tigranes congratulated them. "Let's get positioned."

Finding a log to which they tethered their horses, they selected their places carefully. Gordias was higher on the ridge, Tigranes lower, and Tetius hid behind a boulder on the far side of the road. They strung their bows, selected their best arrows, and settled in to wait.

They waited for about half an hour, with the only traffic being a few horsemen riding by northbound to Jerusalem and an old man on a mule trudging southward. Then they heard it—the pounding of swift hoofs, as if from horses ridden by men anxious to make up for lost time, or to catch an escaping quarry. They braced themselves as three riders came over the rise, the lead one being Hadad. Only three—Tigranes breathed a sigh of relief. He'd not known how many men Hadad would bring, and was confident they could handle as many as five, but he was glad they wouldn't need to.

The murderers rode straight up the center of the road, oblivious to their peril. Tigranes nodded when they got within fifty yards, and they all drew their bows.

"Now!" Tigranes cried, and three arrows flashed through the morning air. The rider on the left was taken through the eye by Gordias' shaft and fell without a sound. Tetius shot the one on the right through the throat, and he fell clutching and gasping. Hadad, distracted by the cry, had half turned, so Tigranes' arrow, which had been intended for his heart, ripped into his left shoulder. With a scream he toppled from his horse.

Tigranes drew his sword and ran out to where Hadad lay writhing in the dust. The arrow was embedded deeply, and bright red blood was surging around the shaft. Tigranes recognized that type of wound—it was mortal. Hadad had minutes to live, if that. Nonetheless, he was struggling to reach his sword hilt.

"Good morning, Hadad," Tigranes said, stepping on his wrist to pin his hand.

Hadad looked up at him with a grimace of pain. "Tigranes!" he spat.

"No," Tigranes replied, reaching down to pluck Hadad's dagger from his belt. "Yusef." He drove the dagger into Hadad's chest, right where Hadad had stabbed the widow's son.

"Good," said Tetius from behind Tigranes. "Three down, clean kills all. Fast work. If you don't mind, Captain, you could grab their horses while we take care of these bodies."

Tigranes, his hands trembling with after-action nerves, clumsily rounded up the riders' horses while Tetius rolled the bodies onto canvas sheets which Gordias had laid out. The two men worked with brisk efficiency, carrying the bodies up the ravine to a stand of scrubby bushes. The bodies were tucked behind these, but not before being stripped of their outer garments and any identifying items. The clothes were stuffed into a bag which would be buried elsewhere. The horses had any distinctive hardware removed from their tack and purged from their saddlebags. Within ten minutes the men were ready to remount, each one leading one of the henchmen's horses.

"What do we do with these?" Tigranes asked as they headed up the road.

"It's too risky to take them ourselves, but if we turn them loose here, they might wander back to Jerusalem. When we get closer to the village, we strip them of all their tack and turn them loose in the fields. We leave the tack by the side of the road for the locals to pick up, and somebody will eventually round up the horses," Tetius explained.

"You seem to have some experience disposing of inconvenient bodies," Tigranes pointed out. "Do I want to know why?"

"If you promise not to ask, cap'n," Tetius said. "I promise not to tell."

"Traffic," Gordias warned, pointing up the road. Three horseman had cleared a curve up ahead and were galloping hard toward them. Tigranes tensed a little, but the horsemen were coming from the direction of Beit-Lechem, not Jerusalem.

"Relax, it's Lord Gaspar," Tetius assured them. Shortly Tigranes could see them more clearly—it was indeed Gaspar and two guards, who galloped up and reined in just in front of them. Gaspar looked suspiciously at the group.

"We got nearly to Beit-Lechem before I noticed you were missing," he said. "Am I to presume those horses have something to do with the security threat that had you so concerned, Captain?"

Tigranes made to answer, but Tetius cut in. "Sorry, my lord. We got to chatting on the road and fell behind, then we chanced upon these stray horses, which we took charge of in hopes of returning to their owners."

Gaspar eyed Tetius warily. "Is this another one of your escapades that I don't want to know about?" he asked in Latin.

"I'm sure I don't know what you're talking about, my lord," Tetius replied in the same tongue.

Gaspar sighed in resignation. "Come on, then. The rest are nearly there."

BEIT-LECHEM

Leaving Gordias and Tetius to bring the horses along, Tigranes and Gaspar galloped to the head of the caravan where Balthazar and Melchior were approaching Beit-Lechem. The three lords looked at each other with quizzical expressions as they realized they hadn't considered one critical question: once they got to Beit-Lechem, what to do then?

Beit-Lechem was a quiet little town that looked just like dozens of other villages they had passed through on their journey. Earth-colored huts clustered around a town square, in which was located the village well. Meadows and harvested fields spread in all directions from the town, and they could see flocks of sheep and goats dotting the hills around. Some of the locals were already poking their heads out of their doors to stare at the column of riders stretching up the Jerusalem road.

"What now?" Gaspar grinned. "Ride to the center of town and start calling out for the son of David?"

"Well, we can't all ride into that town center at the same time no matter what," Balthazar pointed out. It was true—the village square was much too small to hold them all, and even riding through would prove disruptive.

"Let's camp there," Gaspar pointed to a field to their right. "It's been harvested recently, so we won't be disturbing anything." So for the next few hours they pitched their tents and staked the beasts and did all the necessaries for making camp. Some of the locals watched this for a while, but it didn't excite too much notice. Tigranes guessed that the residents of Beit-Lechem were accustomed to groups of travelers passing through on their way to and from Jerusalem. Having a group pitch camp outside town was probably unusual, but not impossible.

Over a late breakfast the magi discussed their next step, and decided to send Tigranes around the village to ask about a child who'd been recently born. Balthazar noticed that Melchior seemed subdued, and suspected he was again struggling with the fear that this would all come to nothing. He'd brightened up a little in Jerusalem after making the decision to proceed to Beit-Lechem, but now that they were here, the sleepy little village didn't look very impressive.

Tigranes left behind all his weapons when he went about the town inquiring. For good measure he took along eager Baba, on the idea that even if a man looked like a soldier, being in the company of a youngster would make him seem less threatening. The magi rested in their pavilion while the men bustled about the business of the camp. There was an air of anticipation—everyone seemed to know that regardless of what they found here, this was the end of the journey.

Tigranes and Baba returned just before noon. "The villagers were slow to open up to me," he explained. "Even though I am a Jew, being an Easterner makes me suspect, and nobody talks too freely to a soldier. But eventually they gave me some information, which led to more.

"There have not been many children born in the village, perhaps two dozen within the past two years. Though a few are newly born, most were born a year or more ago. But there was one—only one—who was born about six months ago."

"When Jupiter and Venus were in conjunction," Balthazar said quietly.

"Yes, my lord," Tigranes confirmed. "The villagers remember that birth especially because of the...unusual circumstances surrounding it."

"Unusual circumstances?" Melchior asked, sitting up a little. "What circumstances?"

"For one thing, my lord, it was just at the time of Caesar's census, so everything was madder than a midsummer bazaar. Everyone had to register in their town of family origin, which gets a bit complex for us Jews, for not all of our ancient cities lie within Judea. But Beit-Lechem does, so Jews from Alexandria to Damascus were trekking here to have their names recorded and pay their denarius."

"Why here?" Gaspar asked.

"Well—towns all over the area, depending on their lineage," Tigranes explained. "Those from the clans of Benjamin would go to Jericho, while the Calebites would go to Hebron, and so on."

"And to Beit-Lechem?"

"Descendants of the house of Jesse, David's father."

The atmosphere in the pavilion tensed a bit. "So," Gaspar said slowly. "One effect of Caesar's order was to bring the descendants of David back to this place."

"Yes, my lord," Tigranes confirmed. "And right in the midst of the confusion, a child was born to one of the families who traveled here."

"Well," grinned Balthazar. "That was poor timing."

"It was worse than that," Tigranes continued. "What few hostels and public houses Beit-Lechem has were jammed, and the homes were full of distant relatives and sundry. People were even renting out their roofs. There was no room anywhere, not even for a woman in labor. They had to send them to the beast's quarters—some huts on the side of a hill east of town."

"And...that's where the child was born? In a barn?" Gaspar asked.

"Apparently so, my lord," Tigranes confirmed.

The magi didn't know whether to laugh or gasp. "Well, that's a memory of the journey to your home town!" Balthazar said. "How strange!"

"And how...unseemly," Melchior added with a note of skepticism. "A birth for a peasant's child, perhaps—but for a long-foretold sovereign? Some might call it an ill omen."

"It gets stranger, my lord," Tigranes replied. "It seems that in the middle of the night that the mother went into labor, several shepherds came into town and began knocking on doors asking where the newborn baby was. With the town full of outsiders this was confusion atop confusion, because nobody knew anything about a newborn baby. Then someone remembered about the woman in labor who'd been sent to the stables, and directed the shepherds there."

"Wait," Gaspar interrupted. "This makes no sense. If the townspeople didn't know about the birth, how did the shepherds know?"

"Well, my lord, that's where it gets...very strange." Tigranes looked reluctant to continue and even a little frightened. "The shepherds spoke of visions in the night, of terrifying heavenly messengers telling them the greatest news they'd ever hear: that just down the hill in Beit-Lechem had been born the *Mesiach*—*Christos* in Greek. Apparently there were a great many messengers, singing the praises of *Hashem* and wishing *shalom*—peaceful harmony—to the men of earth.

"Many of the townspeople thought the shepherds had started drinking their beer a little early. But after they had visited the stables, the shepherds came back through town, assuring everyone that they'd found things just as the heavenly messengers had said, right down to the feeding trough the baby was sleeping in."

Gone was the somnolent air of the warm day. The pavilion fairly crackled with elation, anticipation, and a hint of fear.

Melchior raised his hand, visibly trembling, to his mouth, as if afraid to speak. "And this…this happened about six month ago?"

"Yes, my lord. I confirmed that several times. It was easy for people to remember, because of the census."

"Where did they go?" Melchior asked sharply, grasping Tigranes' arm. "These travelers—when did they leave, and where did they go?"

Tigranes licked his lips, now looking truly frightened. "That's the thing, my lord. They never left. They're still here."

The room grew still with an inexplicable tension, though with an undercurrent of excitement.

"Not…still in the barns, I hope?" asked Balthazar with disbelief.

"No, my lord," Tigranes assured him. "Apparently accommodation was found for them within a couple days of the birth. And when the crowds had ebbed, they were given an old house on the edge of the village, little more than a shack, which was in decrepit condition. But the father is a builder—a *tekton*, as the Greeks would say—and has been working steadily on the abode. It shows signs of recent improvement."

"Wait— 'it shows'? Have you seen this place, Tigranes?" asked Melchior.

"Yes—yes, my lord," Tigranes answered tentatively. "I hope I did not do ill. One of the village women who explained what had happened took me there to show me. It is just on the south side of the village."

"What did you see? What did you do?" Melchior pressed.

"Well, the village woman didn't seem to think there was anything special about the family, so she took us up to the door. It felt strange to be right there and not do anything, so I knocked. A man answered."

"A man? The father, I'm guessing?"

"Yes, my lord. He was a little wary, but friendly enough. I identified myself as your servant, and asked if they would be willing to receive visitors."

"'They'? Did you see anyone else? The child?" Melchior asked.

"Not the child, my lord—he was napping. But I caught a glimpse of the mother. The father was standing at the door talking to me."

"Do these people have names?" Balthazar asked.

"Yes, my lord. The mother is named Miryam—Mary in the Greek form—and the father is Yusef—Joseph."

"Hmm—same as your name," Gaspar said. "And the child?"

"His name is Y'shua, my lord."

"What did he say? What did this—Yusef—say? Will they receive us?" Melchior asked.

"Yes, my lord. He assured me that the child will sleep but a little longer. When he awakes, they will gladly receive you."

The magi looked at each other, stunned and amazed. To come here on no more than a hope and to hear such unexpected, almost conflicting, reports was disconcerting. A child of a kingly line—born to impoverished peasants. A child arriving while Jupiter saluted Venus in the skies—yet not even in his own home. A child whose coming was heralded by heavenly messengers—yet who was born in a barn amidst beasts. How to interpret this tangle of contradictions? Some of the signs seemed to confirm their quest, others seemed to mock it. But the fact that the object of their long journey was near, not half a mile hence, was exhilarating and a little frightening.

"Will...will that be all, my lords?" Tigranes asked hesitantly.

"Yes, yes, for now, Tigranes," Melchior said. "Well done."

"Thank you, my lords," Tigranes bowed and took Baba away from the pavilion.

"It would appear we have reached our goal," Balthazar observed after some silence.

"Yes, yes," Melchior fussed. "But what shall we wear? Court robes seem a little much for the circumstances. What a pity we presented our best gifts to that ape Herod. What shall we bring before him?"

"We'll think of something," Gaspar assured him. "Let us take a little refreshment and talk this over."

After all the anticipation and effort, it seemed a little anticlimactic that all that remained for them to do was go a short way down the road and knock on the door of a hut. But if the numerous signs that had impelled and accompanied their journey were right, then within that hut lay the object of their quest—napping until he awoke, at which time his mother would probably change him. Melchior seemed the most anxious, fussing about the smallest matters. They agreed that their court robes would be far too ostentatious, but neither would it do to come before him clad in their dusty travel garb. In the end Gaspar chose his dress uniform with polished leather and shining breastplate, while Balthazar donned an opulent priestly robe and Melchior wore one of his better long tunics, rich with embroidery.

Then Melchior began fretting about how long they'd waited, and how they didn't wish to intrude, but neither did they wish to keep the family waiting. Finally, Balthazar suggested sending Baba to inquire of the family. He returned within ten minutes to announce that the babe was awake and the family was ready to receive visitors.

The magi had their horses brought, and had Tigranes and Baba lead them through the dusty streets. The party slowed as it approached a small house near the edge of the village. The house still carried some air of abandonment, but showed signs of recent repairs. Fresh plaster dotted the walls here and there, and the door was clearly new, or at least refinished. The trellis that stood on the north side looked newly repaired. The vine-covered lattice was several feet from the house, and from head-height arced to the roof, forming a small but tidy outdoor area that contained a neat little table and some benches—a pleasantly shaded nook for a mother with a baby. The house was clean, but there was no denying that it was old and tiny, the sort of place people would only live in if they could afford nothing better. The magi glanced at each other as they dismounted.

"Has the house of David fallen so far as this?" Balthazar muttered. He thought of all the majestic and imposing edifices he had seen—temples and monuments and palaces that had soared to the sky, awing anyone who beheld them. He remembered one magnificent idol in particular, which had been seated on a great throne and over which had soared an arch painted black and inset with jewels to represent the stars. That had been a far more impressive sight than this shabby cottage.

But then the memory returned of the nights on the observation tower at Melchior's estate, watching the constellations overhead and puzzling about their message. If the signs they had followed to this doorstep were true, then the real stars traversing the heavens had announced the coming of the one who lay behind that door. Balthazar glanced up, toward the blue dome of the sky, and thought of all the stars looking down on them. Suddenly he felt very, very small.

Tigranes approached the door of the house and glanced back at the magi. Melchior nodded, so he knocked gently. The door was opened by a tall man, well into middle age, with curly brown hair and a full beard.

"Ah...sir...Yusef," Tigranes stammered, clearly not having thought out this part. "May I present my masters: Lord Melchior, Lord Balthazar, and Lord Gaspar. They have journeyed from far Parthia to seek an...that is, to meet you—and your... ah... family."

Yusef nodded courteously to the magi and opened the door more widely, beckoning them inside. "My lords are most welcome. Please come in."

The doorway was low enough that the magi had to stoop to enter, especially tall Balthazar. The cottage had only two rooms: a curtained sleeping chamber toward the back and the main room into which they filed. Behind them Yusef motioned Tigranes and Baba inside, where they took up station along the wall beside the door.

In the center of the room, seated on a simple but beautifully crafted bench, sat a young woman—a very young woman. In some ways she looked no different than any other Jewish peasant they'd seen in their travels: olive complexion, dark hair pulled back from her face, average height, clad in simple homespun. Only the white linen veil draped around her head looked anything like finery.

But her eyes—dark like most Jews, they gazed with a steady serenity at the visitors, neither haughty nor cowed, but simply beholding them as they were. Her expression was also serene and open. She was clearly unthreatened by the strangers as well as a little curious.

On her lap sat a child. He was sitting up in his mother's arms looking with bright eyes at the shiny, colorful men who had just come into view, and was waving his small arms in excitement. The boy had curly brown hair and was making gurgling noises. He looked like most babies the magi had ever seen.

The mother made to rise, but Melchior beckoned for her to remain seated.

"My lords, permit me to present my wife Miryam, and her son Y'shua."

The magi bowed slightly and Miryam nodded graciously. "My lords are welcome in our home," she said in a clear voice.

"If my lords will permit," Yusef said. "May we ask why you have sought our threshold?"

"We have come seeking the foretold son of David," Melchior said. "Are you then, sir, of that line? And your son as well?"

Yusef and Miryam glanced at each other before Yusef responded.

"I am indeed of the line of David. The child is as well, but that is by virtue of his mother, who is also of David's house. But he is not my son, save in trust."

The magi looked at each other in mystification, and at the couple, especially the mother, who sat seemingly unperturbed by this scandalous statement. Seeing their consternation, she smiled knowingly and glanced at her husband, who nodded. With no hint of embarrassment or self-consciousness, she began to speak.

"A little over a year ago, I was living in my father's house in Natzaret of the Galil. Yusef and I were betrothed and were awaiting our wedding day. One day, at about the ninth hour, a heavenly messenger came to my room and greeted me with the *shalom* of *Hashem*. He told me that the full favor of the Lord rested upon me, and that I would conceive and bear a son to be named Y'shua. The messenger said this son would be exulted by the Lord's hand, and enthroned upon David's throne, to rule over Ya'akov's house, and that his royal dominion would last forever."

The air in the small room seemed to crackle at her words, and the magi felt their legs tremble.

"The Son of Man," whispered Balthazar, remembering the portion of Bel'Tshazzar's writings that they knew almost by heart.

"Were you, sir, witness to this appearance?" Melchior asked in a quavering voice.

Yusef, who had stepped behind Miryam, smiled gently and shook his head.

"The first I heard of anything unusual was a message from Miryam that her cousin Elisheva was with child and needed assistance, and that she was going to help. Of course, I missed her, but I am accustomed to it. Miryam is always going here and there to help someone.

"When she returned about four months later, she remained in her father's house and did not summon me. I wondered what was happening when the village tongues began wagging that she had returned from her journey with child.

"Now, I know my Miryam, and I know that the sun would rise in the west before she would break any of the Holy Laws. So will say anyone who knows her, including her parents, though that did not silence the village gossips. I admit, I was mystified by her silence, but I waited.

"Then strange and marvelous stories began to circulate about the circumstances of the birth of her cousin Elisheva's son—tales of heavenly messengers in the temple, and mysterious curses miraculously lifted, and glorious prophecies, and a child of great destiny. I wondered that the only person from the village who had witnessed some of these events sat silent in her father's house, reputed to be with child herself. The more I pondered these matters, the more I trembled at what might be afoot in Israel. I will speak plainly, my lords: I was frightened. I am but a simple Israelite, a sinful man like every other. What have I to do with such wondrous events?"

The magi, in the grip of an awe that deepened with every minute, nodded in understanding.

"I became so frightened that I had nearly decided to leave—to send Miryam quiet word breaking our betrothal, that she might remain in her father's house and not suffer from gossips at our wedding or anywhere else. But then the messenger came and told me otherwise."

"The…messenger?" Melchior asked.

"Yes, my lord—in a dream," Yusef replied. "He confirmed my fears: that the child whom Miryam bore was of the Lord and not of any man. It was clear to me that great events were in motion in which I played but a small role. I grew even more certain that I should make myself scarce, but the messenger told me that I should take Miryam as my wife and provide for the child as my own. So, frightening though it was, I did."

"Two messengers," muttered Melchior, then turned to Miryam. "My lady, my lady—the messenger who came to you, when did he come? What time of year?"

"It would have been a year ago Tishri, near the time of the Sukkoth festival."

"About the time of the equinox," Balthazar explained in a whisper. "Just when Jupiter approached Regulus in Leo."

"So the birth was six months ago now," Melchior continued.

"Yes, my lord," Miryam smiled a little as she confirmed this basic arithmetic, but the magi nodded with even more excitement.

"And this messenger to your house, my lady," Melchior pressed, though visibly hesitant. "This messenger—forgive me, but I must ask—did he...come to you?"

Miryam and Yusef glanced at one another in puzzlement, then understanding dawned and Miryam smiled slightly. The other two magi knew the import of the question. There were many legends of the gods coming to human women and impregnating them. The offspring of these unions were heroes and the like, half mortal and half divine. It was important to know who this messenger had been, and what had been the nature of his message.

"Not in that manner, my lord," Miryam explained. "He remained across the room from me. When I asked how this wonder he announced would come to pass, the messenger said that the *Ruach HaKodesh* would blanket me and conceive the child within me."

"*Ruach HaKodesh?*" Melchior asked.

"Literally the Divine Breath, my lord," Yusef translated. "Also known as the Holy Spirit, the Divine Presence."

"So, you were not touched?"

"Not in that sense, my lord. I was then as I remain to this day: a virgin."

Balthazar's eyes grew wide and he began visibly trembling. "Virgo," he whispered, sinking to his knees. The others swiftly followed, but Balthazar knew better than any of them the significance of this.

The Divine Child. The Virgin-Born. Legends were laced with hints and glimmers of One who would spring not from the loins of men, or even gods, but from the benevolent favor of the Highest God. There were many tales of how this Divine Child would come—found beside a riverbank, hatched from a golden egg, or simply appearing among men—but His coming always heralded a new age upon earth, a time of grace and harmony.

It was all aligning. The signs in the skies. The ancient writings. The coming of the heavenly messengers. Now this: a virginal conception. It did not occur to any of them to doubt this word. That this couple was speaking the plain truth was clear from their simple, honest faces. Even the magi, who were merely hearing these accounts, knew that they were in the presence of such powerful truth that lies and fancies and other human vanities were demolished like sandcastles before a flood tide. How much more this simple couple to whom these events had actually happened? The weight of the truth hung in the air and trembled in the ground and turned their bones to water.

The Divine Child. The Promised One. The hope of every people on earth. Gaspar did not lift his eyes to the Babe, but he did see Yusef standing there, and the incongruity struck him. This one unarmed man was all the protection this child had. By rights the family should be sheltered in a strong fortress with legions stationed all around. Where was the safety in a tumbledown hut on the outskirts of an unwalled village? Surely the Divine could guard His Child more adequately than this?

But as Gaspar looked at the builder, who was standing to the side and a little behind the mother and Child, his vision seemed to clear. He still saw the same strong peasant man looking down fondly at his little family, but it was like he could also see the man's heart. Here, Gaspar saw, was a man who had no concern for his own honor. Here was a man willing to pour out every ounce of his strength for the sake of those entrusted to him. Here was a man who was willing to fade into the background, eclipsed by this Child and even his wife, in order to support the divine plan.

Here was true manhood. Here was true strength.

Gaspar thought he had seen strength. He had seen legates send their legions into battle with a wave of their hands, and had thought that strength. He had heard the shock of armies clashing on the battlefield, and had thought that strength. He had even seen the emperor on the rostrum while ranks of legionaries marched by, and had thought that strength.

But he had known all these men, too—the legates and the officers and the governors. Beneath the pomp and posturing they were all the same. Though they claimed they were working for the glory of Rome or their kingdom or their family, they were ultimately seeking their own glory thereby, to make a name for themselves. All their strength was devoted to that end.

But not this peasant builder. For most men, the path to establishing their name on the earth was to marry, sire children, and raise the children up to honor their father's memory. This man had had his wife taken from him, thus having this usual path cut off by divine intervention. Yet he had not complained—in fact, he had cooperated willingly. This man so desired the good that this Child would bring about that he was willing to fade into obscurity to see it happen.

Some would call that folly. Gaspar saw that it was strength, strength like he'd never seen in all his travels, strength that he'd almost despaired of ever seeing. Abruptly he stood, stepped over before Yusef, drew his sword, and knelt at his feet, proffering the sword in gesture of fealty.

"My lord," said Gaspar. "I pledge you my sword, my strength, and my full loyalty, if you will have it."

If Yusef was startled by this gesture, he gave no sign of it. Without comment he took the blade and turned it in his hands.

"This blade has seen much use over many years, has it not, my lord?" Yusef asked.

"It has, my lord," Gaspar replied.

"I accept your service, and return to you your sword under these conditions," Yusef said. "You must never use it to shed innocent blood. You must never use it to exult yourself. And you must always use it for justice, especially for the protection of those weaker than you. My lord, take back your sword."

"As you will, my lord," Gaspar looked up as Yusef lay the sword across his outstretched hands. What had he done? Pledged himself to this stranger? Now his liege? His liege—he must have a gift for his liege…then he remembered.

"Baba!" Gaspar called over his shoulder.

"Yes, my lord?"

"In my left saddlebag, at the bottom! The small heavy leather sack—bring it to me!"

"Yes, my lord!" Baba said, dashing out. He was back in a minute and handed the purse to Gaspar.

"My lord," Gaspar said from his knees, holding the bag of gold up to Yusef. "Receive this as a token of my esteem and a pledge of my service."

Yusef nodded gravely and accepted the sack. Somewhat surprised by its weight, he looked inside and his eyes widened.

"My lord," Yusef protested, making to return the gift. But Gaspar was on his feet, holding out his hands in refusal.

"No, my lord, it is yours. It was given to me, but it was never mine. I have always known that. Now I know for whom I have been carrying it."

Yusef looked at him calmly, weighing the sack in his hand, then nodded gravely. "Thank you, my lord."

Balthazar barely noticed this byplay. He was kneeling on the dirt floor of the house, struggling to absorb what he was in the presence of. The Divine Child? Was *that* whom they had been seeking? But…to the Jews? How would that work? Would the whole world become Jews?

Awed and confused, he lifted his eyes to find the mother, Miryam, looking at him kindly, as if she could see the turmoil in his heart. She was young, so very young—but where had youth learned such depth and serenity?

The wife of a god, that's what she was. No, the wife of *the* God, the Jewish God, the One God of heaven and earth. Not taken and bedded like the fancy of some lustful Olympian, but breathed upon, that the Child might be formed in a virginal womb.

Pure worship—from the very start. *Pure* worship, the Rock uncut by human hands.

Human hands.

Balthazar lifted his hands and looked at them. He alone knew the full tale of where these hands had been, and what they had done. No other man knew all those stories, not even his closest companions. Oh, he'd speak of his quest for the spiritual, and tell stories of the places he had visited and the things he had seen. But he never spoke of the terrible details of some of those visits—the gruesome initiations and the horrid rituals and the profane rites. He had embraced all that in the name of the search for truth, but now it all came flooding back, and with it the awareness that he had been indulging perverse curiosity. These hands—these hands had participated in black deeds, horrid deeds that any decent man would have turned away from in revulsion. He raised them slowly and stared, as if expecting to see them stained and dripping with gore and filth.

"My lord," a calm voice broke through his dark reverie. "May I see your hands?"

Balthazar shook his head, disoriented. "My lady?"

Miryam glanced over her shoulder at Yusef, who nodded in response. She lifted the baby into his arms and turned back to Balthazar, her hands extended. "Your hands, my lord. May I see them?"

Even at the superficial level of social protocol, Balthazar recoiled. A married woman, a Jewess at that, touching a strange man, especially a Gentile? But her husband was standing right there, and apparently had given her permission. The usual conventions did not seem to apply in this house.

But it was the deeper level that most alarmed Balthazar. She wanted to see his hands? He didn't want to see his own hands! He wanted to hide his hands, his face, his whole being! He wasn't fit company for common soldiers, much less the wife of a god and the mother of the Holy Child!

"My...hands, my lady?" he replied clumsily, trying to tuck them away into the folds of his robe.

"Yes, my lord—by your kind permission," Miryam replied, holding out her hands expectantly.

Now Balthazar was caught between the guilt and shame that was overwhelming him and the knowledge that he could not refuse this woman. He knew with certainty that her least wish would be to him like a command from heaven. There was nothing he would not do for her, no request of hers he could possibly deny.

But she was asking to see his hands.

Tremulously he drew his hands out, half expecting them to steam and stink and drip filth onto her lap. With reluctance he extended them, but when she reached for them he started to pull them away out of fear that the purity of her touch would scald him. Giving him a look of gentle admonishment, she held out her hands until he gingerly placed his palms on hers.

Her hands did not burn, but were cool and gentle. Her skin was a bit rough and calloused like any peasant woman's would be, but her touch was light. She stroked his hands, front and back, turning them over in hers and examining them. Balthazar dropped his eyes in shame, certain that this woman who had received heralds from heaven could see every blotch, every stain of each sin he had committed with those hands.

"You have strong hands, my lord," Miryam said calmly. "Hands that were made for great things."

"My lady," Balthazar choked, shaking his head and trembling. He lifted his eyes just until he could see her hands. "My lady, you should not…if only you knew—"

"My lord," Miryam interrupted. When he kept his eyes downcast she shook his hands and said more firmly, "My lord, listen to me." Reluctantly he lifted his eyes to hers, tears pouring down his face. Her dark eyes gazed back with calm and wisdom far beyond her years, and he knew that, somehow, she had indeed seen all his wretched history—or all that mattered. But her gaze held no shock or revulsion or condemnation, but rather acceptance and understanding and even—pity?

"Dwell on that no longer, my lord," she assured him in a quiet voice. "It is past, and soon will be washed away completely. Walk those paths no more. Take back your hands, and never again lift them in the service of idols." Gently she folded his hands and returned them to him.

Stunned, Balthazar held up his hands and gazed at them in wonder. With the same surety that he had known of their defilement, he now knew beyond question that they were clean. No, more than just clean—fresh and purified, as new as the hands of the baby seated in his father's arms. The tears continued to stream down as he gasped and sobbed. "My lady, my lady."

"Know *shalom*, my lord. Your search is at an end."

Wiping his blurred eyes with his sleeve, he looked up to see her favoring him with a broad, loving smile—a mother's smile. Still flexing and wringing his hands in disbelief, he knew what he could do. It would only be a pittance against what she had done for him, but he could do this at least.

"Baba!"

"Yes, my lord?"

"There is a sack hanging from my saddlebow. In it is a wooden box—bring the box to me."

"Yes, my lord!"

Puzzled, Miryam took the baby back from Yusef and settled him in her lap. Baba returned shortly and handed Balthazar the box as if it was a head of cabbage, oblivious to the value of what lay within.

"My lady," Balthazar bowed low where he knelt and held the box out to her. "This is but a small token of what I would lay at your feet, but it is the best I have to offer."

"Your presence is gift enough to our home, my lord," Miryam answered graciously. She opened the box, deftly maneuvering it to keep the baby's eager hands from scattering the brown and golden crystals therein. Yusef leaned over to peer at the contents, and they both looked a little mystified.

"It's myrrh, my lady," Balthazar explained. Miryam's eyes lifted, but Yusef's eyes grew wide and he gasped.

"My lord," he stammered. "That much! We cannot—"

"Please, my lord," Balthazar pleaded. "Do not refuse me. It is a small thing to me, especially in light of what—of what—" But his eyes were again filling and his throat was constricting, and he could not go on. He rose to his feet and backed away, bowing, seeking a corner in which he could regain his composure.

From where he knelt on the floor, Melchior could tell there were things going on to his left. Gaspar was holding some conversation with the father, then Balthazar was somehow dealing with the mother—which Melchior mostly noticed because she moved the babe for a minute. All these things were happening but feet from him, but he attended them not. He had eyes for only one thing.

The Child.

Melchior felt like he could not stop staring, but he didn't know what he was looking for. Had he expected the Holy Child to glow? To be translucent? To levitate, or speak, or perform some other incredible deed? How ludicrous. What would a child be, but a child, doing what a child would do? Slowly it dawned on him that his unexamined expectations presumed that a Divine Child would be more divine than child, and therefore would somehow manifest divine attributes. But according to the mother, Miryam, she had borne this baby in the usual way of women. The conception was divine, but everything else was typical of humanity.

How could that possibly be? Was the Divine Child both divine and human? But the gods dwelt in the high spheres, in realms of pristine purity and beauty, that knew not death or decay. No—this was the Jewish God, who claimed to be Lord of all the heavens and earth, and creator of all within them. Why, that was even higher and further removed! How could such a being come down to this world, into the dust and sweat and muck and spittle? How could a god partake of the toil and pain and futility and frustration that was man's lot?

Not to mention the death.

The death?

How could this be? The gods were immortal. That was part of what made them gods. This was especially true of the Jewish God, who claimed to be the source of being for all the lesser gods such as the messengers sent to Bel'Tshazzar.

And this woman and her husband.

What was the nature of this Divine Child? How divine was he? And how human? Melchior had to know. Hot urgency surged within him. He must know all he could about this baby! He felt like the whole purpose of his life, of the entire world, was somehow bound up with this mysterious child.

"My...my lady," Melchior stammered.

"Yes, my lord?"

"Forgive my presumption, but...but I must know."

"Ask what you will, my lord."

"This child—he was carried in the normal manner? To a full term?"

"Yes, my lord," Miryam replied with a quiet smile.

"And delivered—as children always are?"

"Yes, my lord," Miryam assured him. "Though the birth circumstances were unusual, and I had no attendants but Yusef here, the child came as children always do."

"But the messenger told you..."

"That he would be called son of the Highest, and that he would be given the Throne of his ancestor David, and that his kingdom would never end," Miryam said calmly, as if with long practice.

"Yes, yes, the Son of Man, everlasting dominion," Melchior muttered, recalling Bel'Tshazzar's vision. "Clearly divine. And you, my lord? The messenger said?"

"That he was conceived of *Ruach HaKodesh*, and that he would save his people from their sins," Yusef added.

"Divine, divine," Melchior continued. "And yet—so human. My lady, if I may be so bold, does the babe eat, and sleep, and...do all that babies do?"

"Yes, my lord," Miryam assured him with a broad smile.

"And—even bleed?"

Miryam glanced at Yusef, then nodded. "When he underwent *b'rit-milhah* according to *Torah*, he bled and cried, though he healed quickly," she explained.

Melchior gasped quietly. "Then he is in every way human?"

"It would seem so, my lord," Miryam confirmed.

"If—if I may be so bold, my lady, my lord—may I see him? In his simple humanity? Not to doubt your testimony, but that I might behold with my own eyes." Melchior bowed his face to the ground in the manner of the lowest supplicant.

Behind him Gaspar and Balthazar were wide-eyed at the audacity of the request. Miryam's eyes widened a little, but she glanced over her shoulder at Yusef, who nodded calmly. With a practiced hand she undid little Y'shua's wraps and held him naked on her lap, wiggling and cooing. The magi gazed at the perfect, yet plainly human, little form.

"Just like us," Melchior whispered, his hand lifting toward the child but not quite daring to reach for him.

"You may touch him, my lord," Miryam assured him, sensing his hesitation. "He will come to no harm by your hand."

His aged fingers trembling, Melchior reached to gently graze the baby's shoulder. Y'shua watched him, making little infant gasps all the while. As Melchior drew his hand back, the baby caught one of his fingers and held it briefly.

"If I may, my lord, my lady?" Balthazar's voice came over Melchior's shoulder. Melchior stood and withdrew to give his companion a chance to kneel and touch the baby's leg. "The Divine Child."

"And yet human in every detail," Melchior said. "What wonder is this?"

"What wonder, indeed, my lord," Miryam added quietly. "At times we are in awe ourselves." Yusef nodded agreement.

Now Balthazar was bowing his head to the floor, then rising to make room for Gaspar to do his obeisance. Fierce excitement was welling up within Melchior, and seeing in Yusef's hands the sack which Gaspar had given, he was reminded of something.

"Baba!"

"Yes, my lord?"

"In my right saddlebag, toward the back, there is an embroidered bag. You will recognize it by the scent. Fetch it for me!"

"Yes, my lord!"

Miryam was smiling indulgently as Gaspar's strong soldier's hands barely touched the baby's arm. Then he bowed and stood as she bundled the baby up again. The child started a little as Baba came breathlessly through the door, holding the bag. Melchior took it and checked the contents, though the aroma was confirmation enough. Kneeling at Miryam's feet, he bowed and held out the open sack to the child.

"My lady, my lord, we are but men who thought we knew much, but before this wonder we stand silenced. But this we do know: this was offered to an idol in a wealthy temple in a bustling city far from here. We are pleased to lay it at the feet of the true God in this simple house."

"We thank you, my lord," Miryam replied with grave dignity, taking the bag. She let the baby play with the pale crystals a bit before handing the sack to Yusef. He sniffed the contents and felt the crystals with a puzzled expression.

"It is frankincense from Sheba, my lord," Balthazar explained, guessing that a builder from the Galil would not recognize it on sight.

Yusef's eyes widened again. "My lord..." he gasped in protest, but the magi had all risen and were backing away.

"By your kind permission," Melchior said. "We will take our leave now. If we may call again at your convenience?"

"My lords are always welcome in our home," Miryam said with a courteous nod. The lords bowed deeply and backed out the door.

Dazed and drained, the men stepped out into the bright sunlight. It was early afternoon, and they were standing on the same road that they'd taken to get here, their horses stamping and swishing their tails in the midday warmth. It seemed impossible that they had started that day before dawn in Jerusalem. Their early departure, their stay in the city, their entire journey seemed like something that had happened an age ago on the other side of the world. There was the same sun in the sky and the same ground beneath their feet, but it seemed all different now. Everything was changed. In one sense, everything they had thought they knew lay broken and scattered at their feet, but in another, the world seemed renewed. They gazed about in wonder. The light seemed brighter, the air cleaner, the clouds overhead whiter—it was like everything had been created anew while they were within the house.

"We shall have a feast," Melchior announced. "We shall have a memorable feast to celebrate the successful completion of our journey. Tigranes!"

"Yes, my lord?"

"Is there somewhere we can obtain a heifer to roast?"

"I imagine so, my lord," Tigranes answered. "Beit-Lechem is a farming village."

"Then find two."

"Two heifers, my lord? That would be enough to feed the entire village!"

"That's the intention," Melchior smiled. "How about wine and dates and other delicacies? Can we find those?"

"Possibly, my lord, but in large quantities we might have to return to Jerusalem, and there is a complication with that."

"What complication?"

"We would have to move quickly. There are only a few hours of daylight remaining before *Shabbat*, the Holy Day. Once the sun sets there is no buying or selling, especially in Jerusalem. But with fast camels we may be able to make it to the city in time."

"Then make haste, Captain. Consult with the head cook, take whomever you need, but have those supplies by sunset," Melchior instructed.

"Yes, my lord," Tigranes bowed. "Baba, come!" They raced off about their errand, leaving the magi standing in the road, still amazed at the events of the day.

"Feasting the entire village?" Gaspar asked with a raised eyebrow.

"Can you think of a better reason?" Melchior asked. They looked back at the simple hut.

"I wonder if they realize there's enough wealth in that hut to buy all Beit-Lechem?" Balthazar mused.

"My friend," Melchior answered in an awed whisper. "There is enough wealth in that hut to buy the entire world."

FLIGHT

While the magi retired to their pavilion to rest and meditate, their camp broke into feverish activity to comply with Melchior's orders. Quantities were swiftly calculated and two assistant cooks dispatched to Jerusalem within the hour to procure supplies, with Baba along to keep the three camels under control. The village rabbi was consulted and, after an interview with the head cook, announced that the foreign dignitaries were familiar enough with Jewish dietary laws to prepare a kosher feast for the village. Two lucky farmers were paid handsomely for tender heifers not a year old, which were slaughtered under the rabbi's supervision. Local stores of wheat, figs, eggs, and other edibles also found a market as the head cook bustled about, rattling off orders and pulling his hair. Finally, as the sun dipped toward the horizon, the mission to Jerusalem returned in triumph, the camels laden with almost everything they had been sent for: wine, oil, dates, honey, fish, oranges, and the rest. Now the head cook felt confident of being able to prepare the feast he had envisioned—which only sent him into further paroxysms of anxiety.

The magi slept peacefully that night, but their cooking crew was up before dawn, starting preparations by torchlight. Fires were kindled in two pits, great spits rigged, and by sunup the two heifers were turning over the flames while men were pressed into service grinding flour, shelling nuts, and mixing ingredients for mysterious dishes. A makeshift oven was constructed and dough was set to rising. Baba was nearly run ragged carrying the head cook's orders to all the busy helpers and reporting problems back.

In midmorning the village's synagogue assembly took place, with Tigranes in attendance as the envoy on the magi's behalf. The synagogue leaders welcomed him cordially, especially in light of the generous donation he brought from the magi. In their name he extended an invitation to the entire village to come to the feast, which would commence just after noon.

After the synagogue assembly most of the families pretended to go home, but the tantalizing aromas around the stranger's camp proved too compelling. First little children, then young men and women, and finally entire families came out to watch the preparations. Though the villagers were restricted as to what work they could perform on *Shabbat*, no such constraint bound the busy Gentiles, and it was clear they were preparing a magnificent feast. *Shabbat* feasts were always welcome, and *Shabbat* feasts which others paid for and prepared were even better.

At last the cook announced all was ready, and Tigranes summoned the rabbi and village elders. When the head cook had assured the rabbi that all the food had been prepared properly, the *b'rakah* was made and the feast commenced. Savory meat was sliced and stuffed into fresh bread, sweet dates were munched, citrus juice dribbled down eager little chins, and wine flowed. Soldiers entranced village lads and lasses with tales of fierce danger in faraway lands. Parents let their children stuff themselves, figuring it would be long before they tasted such delicacies again. Village musicians fetched instruments and struck up some lively tunes, and soon the locals were teaching the exotic *goyim* proper Jewish dancing.

The magi took no part in any of this. As soon as they got word that the little family had returned to their home from the synagogue assembly, the magi rode over with baskets prepared by the cook to have a private feast. They were welcomed warmly and hosted in the shaded side yard beneath the trellis. The fare the magi brought was the richest the little house had ever seen, but Miryam insisted on adding to it the freshly baked *Shabbat* bread which had been rising all night. To the magi, it seemed the finest bread they had ever eaten.

So as the village celebrated, the magi and the family whiled away the afternoon in peaceful company. Miryam taught the childless bachelors how to hold a baby, and they took turns with little Y'shua in their laps, letting him play with the trinkets they wore around their necks. They told the tale of their journey: the signs they'd seen in the heavens, the prophetic writings, their hopes for what they would find, the struggles they had endured. Yusef and Miryam told of the wonders that had surrounded the events of the birth. They spoke of Miryam's cousin Elisheva and her husband Z'kharyah the priest; the wondrous vision he had seen in the temple and the curse that had been pronounced on him, the unexpected pregnancy and birth of the foretold little Yochanan, and the lifting of the curse on Z'kharyah, and his subsequent prophecy of redemption. The magi sat amazed as the couple told of the night of Y'shua's birth, under those terrible conditions, and the visit of the shepherds with the tales of the heavenly messengers. They told of their visit to the temple where they had met the aged prophet who had been assured he would see *Mesiach* before his death, and how the prophet had told them that Y'shua was the one, and had spoken great prophecies over him. By the time they were finished, the magi were comprehending with awe that tremendous things were moving in heaven and on earth, of which they were only a small part.

At one point in the afternoon, when Miryam had taken the child inside for a rest, Gaspar got the chance to ask about something that had been nagging him. "We were glad to find you here, Lord Yusef, but it does raise the question: if you are from Natzaret in the Galil, and only came to Beit-Lechem because of the census, how comes it that you are still here all these months later? Why did you not go home?"

"There were two reasons, my lord, one very practical and one—deeper. Practically, we could not move too soon after the baby was born, for obvious reasons. Though helpful townsfolk found us suitable lodging quickly, we were pinned here until Miryam and Y'shua were able to travel. Then we learned of a village man who had inherited this house when his childless aunt and uncle died. They hadn't been able to maintain it in their final years, so it had fallen into disrepair and he could not rent it to anyone. He heard of our plight, and graciously offered to let us live here if I fixed it up while we did so. He has provided the materials and I have provided the labor. Now I am all but finished—only a few details remain—but it would have been ungrateful of us to leave with the work half done."

"So, once the house is finished, will you then return home?"

"That brings up the other, deeper reason for our remaining. Since those first messages in Natzaret, neither Miryam nor I have received any direct instructions about the child. Even the word about the census took us by surprise, but we had to obey like everyone else. Only after we had been here a few weeks did it occur to us that the Lord had arranged matters so that not only was the child born in the Holy Land, but in the city of his ancestors.

"That got us wondering. The rabbis teach that of all the patriarchs, only Yitzchak son of Avraham, the child of promise, lived his entire life within the bounds of the Holy Land. Was that the intention for this Child of Promise as well? We did not know, and without further instructions did not wish to guess. And after the prophecies pronounced over him at the temple, we were even more reluctant to move without instructions. So we have lingered, waiting."

Eventually the peaceful, joyous day drew to a close. The magi took their leave of Yusef, Miryam, and little Y'shua to retire to their camp. Sated villagers bid farewell to their new friends and returned to their homes carrying whatever was left over from the feast. The cook and his crew had long since collapsed in their tents, exhausted but satisfied with the results of their efforts. Everyone else slept where they could, and Tigranes set only a light watch, mostly to keep the scavengers away.

The stars wheeled overhead, the moon traced his path across the night sky, and Beit-Lechem slumbered. In their pavilion the magi slept soundly. But in the darkest hour of the night, long past midnight but before dawn had begun to lighten the eastern sky, the three men stirred, then suddenly sat bolt upright in the darkness, looking about in alarm.

"He's not finished," Gaspar said in an ice-cold voice. "Guard! Torches!"

The other two magi sat silent, still trembling. Balthazar especially felt weak. It was one thing to study the ancients like Bel'Tshazzar and their accounts of messages delivered in dreams, or even to hear men like Yusef speak of them. But to have a heavenly messenger come to your own dreams, to hear him speak in a voice that melted your insides, was the most terrifying experience any of the magi had ever had.

The younger Gaspar recovered more quickly. He was outside the pavilion snapping off orders, seemingly intent on waking the entire camp.

"Tigranes!"

"Yes, my lord!" Tigranes answered, stumbling from his tent as he pulled on his tunic.

"Take Baba and run to the house. Ascertain the safety of the family and send Baba back with word. Stand guard at the house until I come or send reinforcements."

"Yes, my lord," Tigranes said, grabbing a torch and turning to go.

"Tigranes!" Gaspar said. "Go armed!"

"Yes, my lord!"

Baba had already been roused by the spreading tumult in the camp, so he held a torch while Tigranes swiftly donned his weapons. Then they ran to the house, which lay quiet in the starlight. Baba stood to one side with the torch while Tigranes tapped on the door.

"Who is it?" came the swift reply, a man's sharp whisper. There was nothing sluggish or sleepy about that response— Yusef had been awake.

"It is I, my lord—Tigranes. I'm here with Baba at Lord Gaspar's command. Is everyone all right?"

The door flung open and Yusef looked out warily. Behind him the house was dimly lit with an oil lamp, and Tigranes could see Miryam moving about with quiet determination.

"We are well, but I have received another message in a dream. Herod—the child is in danger. We must flee now— tonight!"

Baba gasped but Tigranes nodded. "I think something must have happened with the lords. A dream would explain it. The camp was quiet, then suddenly all was astir in their pavilion. Lord Gaspar told me nothing, but sent me here with all haste. I am to report back to him and set an armed guard to insure your safety."

Yusef nodded grimly. "The lords' assistance is appreciated, but we cannot tarry. We hope to be on our way by dawn."

"We will not hinder you, and will help as we may," Tigranes said. "But where will you go? Jerusalem is no safer, and Herod's arm reaches into the Galil."

"Neither," Yusef shook his head. "The messenger was clear: we must go to Egypt and seek shelter there."

"How will you travel? Afoot?"

"For now. Thanks to the lords, we will be able to purchase a beast soon, but right now we must get away."

"The lords will help. Baba: go and report to the lords all we have said. Say that I recommend we give them a pack donkey at least, if not two."

"Yes, Captain," Baba said, rushing away.

"Be about your preparations, my lord," Tigranes said. "I will stand guard out here."

Back at the camp Baba reported everything to the magi. All about them was the bustle of a camp being hastily packed up by torchlight.

"So Yusef received a message as well," Balthazar said. "Egypt! It's a long, dangerous road."

"It's only really dangerous along the first part," Gaspar assured him. "The south road from here skirts the Negev, which can harbor bandits and brigands. But it joins the Gaza Road just before the Egyptian border. That's an important road for commerce, so the Romans keep it well patrolled. They should be safer once they're on that."

"Can they get to that sooner without taking this south road?" Balthazar asked.

"Not without going back toward Jerusalem, which is the last thing they want to do."

"So what should we do? Escort them?" Melchior asked.

"Not by my counsel," Gaspar replied. "Herod's eyes are upon us. He sent us with instructions, and we're the only ones he knows about—he doesn't yet know about them. The heavenly messenger told us not to return to Herod, so our only question is which route we should take. Of all the options, we cannot take any route that keeps us close to the family. We need to draw his eyes after us, not them."

"Which route do you recommend?" Balthazar asked. "You know this region better than any of us."

"From here the major roads lead south and north," Gaspar mused as if thinking aloud. "We don't want to go south and west, since that's the route the family will be taking. But south and east, around the Salt Sea, takes us through Idumea, where Herod would have many spies. North is out of the question, for that takes us to Jerusalem, but even northwest, skirting the city, gets us into the Judean hills. The roads are tortured there, and we would be long delayed right within Herod's grasp. Perhaps the coastal road, if we were swift—or maybe..." Gaspar paused, as if thinking furiously.

"Maybe what?" Balthazar prodded after a minute.

"Maybe by sea?" Gaspar offered. "We could head due west from here until we strike the main road between Jerusalem and Gaza, and then northwest to the port of Joppa. We could take ship there and go to Seleucia, the port of Antioch in Syria."

"Hiring a ship large enough to take all this would drain our resources severely," Balthazar advised, sweeping his arm around at the men and beasts and supplies. "We still have to travel back to the East."

"We can tarry in Antioch and figure all that out," Gaspar replied dismissively. "We just need to get away from here quickly."

"So that takes care of us," Melchior said. "But what of them? Are they to traverse the desert alone and unguarded, bearing the treasure they do?"

"I have an idea about that," Gaspar assured him. "But I must speak to Tigranes about it—if you can spare him."

As the sun rose over the hills, the residents of Beit-Lechem awoke to a surprise: the camp of the Gentile lords, which had seemed to be pitched for a long stay, was completely gone. The field in which they'd camped was empty of all but the typical debris left by a group of people swiftly departing. The fire pits from the feast were cold ashes, and the grass was trampled and crushed, but there was neither man nor beast to be seen. Nobody knew where the Gentiles had gone.

None of the townsfolk yet noticed that the humble hut to the south of town was also vacant. As soon as there was sufficient light for travel, a man leading two donkeys had set out on the south road, the chancy route that led toward Hebron, Beer-Sheva, and eventually the Egyptian border. One of the donkeys was laden with bundles and bags—all the worldly possessions of a small family. The other donkey bore a woman holding a sleeping baby. The man was accompanied by a youngster of perhaps a dozen years, trudging wearily as if his night's sleep had been interrupted.

Before the little party had gone out of sight, another group set out along the same road. These travelers were also on foot, though they had a sole pack horse. They were half a dozen men-at-arms walking casually, not in formation. They bore swords, but their shields, spears, and archery gear were strapped to the horse—though loosely, as if for quick access if needed. They ambled along about half a mile behind the family, not so close as to appear to be escorting them, but close enough to be able to move in quickly if anything threatened.

Tigranes was leading the hastily assembled band of guards, many of whom were nursing sore heads in the aftermath of the feast. He didn't like this arrangement. He would have preferred a stronger guard in closer attendance about the family, especially considering how much wealth they had secreted away in those shabby bundles. But Gaspar had argued that too large a guard would actually draw attention, so they'd compromised on this ruse—what appeared to be a band of soldiers traveling the Hebron road on their way to their next assignment, which would just happen to stay behind the family at a suitable distance to move up if some threat materialized. Tigranes was still nervous about this, for he knew threats could materialize so quickly that even being within sight of the family might not afford enough time to respond. So Gaspar had suggested having the fleet Baba travel with the family, ready to dash back for aid should the need arise. That had been the best they could arrange.

The plan was that this loose escort would tail the family to the Egyptian border, where Yusef and Miryam could join up with one of the many bands of travelers making for the populous Nile delta—ideally a group of Jews, who liked to travel together. Once they were safely on their way, the guard would turn back along the coastal road and make their way to Joppa, where they'd find a ship to take them to Antioch where the magi would be waiting. Given the pace the family could sustain, Tigranes guessed that they had four or five days until they reached the border.

He'd be very glad when they did.

For his part, Baba was having as good a time as could be expected. The thrill of being awakened in the night to be sent dashing about on critical errands was fading in the subsequent exhaustion, but noon was approaching and they would soon seek shelter for the blazing midday hours. In the meantime the Lord Yusef and the Lady Miryam were good company. It felt strange to call them that, for by their clothing and accents they appeared to be village peasants of the type that the folk of the estate back home—such as his mother and father—would look down upon. But there clung to them a dignity and nobility that raised them above their simple state. Besides, Baba had seen with his own eyes all three lords—who had stood in the presence of kings and high priests—bow with their faces to the ground before this couple and their child. That was what was done before emperors! If the high lords so honored this family, should not he, simple Baba, at least call them lord and lady despite their appearances?

But Baba quickly forgot their exalted status, for talking with them was easy. Lord Yusef didn't say much, but when he spoke his words were simple and kind. Lady Miryam was more conversational, though she did more listening than talking. She asked Baba questions about his family and his travels and all the things he'd learned, and then listened with interest as he rambled on. She never seemed impatient or irritated, even when the sun grew hot or the baby grew fussy. They had to stop a couple of times to feed the baby. Lady Miryam was happy to let Baba help as he could, even allowing him to hold the baby when the adults needed to arrange things.

As noon approached, Baba scouted ahead and found a broad wadi that was large enough for both the family and the escort. Lord Yusef led the donkeys further into the gully until they found a north-facing wall with a good overhang. To this he quickly rigged a makeshift canopy to provide shade, and arranged the bags into a bed for Lady Miryam and little Y'shua. They dozed through the hottest part of the day while Lord Yusef sat with his back to the rock and nodded. Baba sat in the shade of a scrubby bush and tried to keep watch, but his eyelids were heavy, too. At least the guards who were taking their midday rest up near the mouth of the wadi were within calling range.

When the worst heat had passed, they got back on the road and plodded along, with occasional stops, until the sun drew close to the horizon. The two parties camped close together, not sharing a campsite but pitching their sites adjacent to each other. Travelers often clustered in this way at night, so this would not draw undue notice.

So the tedious journey continued for days. Since none of them had traveled this road before, nobody had any idea how far it was to the border. They knew they were on the proper road because it took them through the larger towns of Hebron and Beer-Sheva, as well as the occasional smaller village. But once south of Beer-Sheva, the road ran through the featureless expanse of the Negev. They only saw two other groups of travelers—one swift-moving band of northbound riders who dashed by in a flurry of dust, paying neither party any heed, and another caravan of camels and donkeys that was traveling so slowly that even the family passed them. Tigranes exchanged courtesies with the caravan master, who affirmed that they were still on the correct road, though he could not tell how much further they had to travel to reach the border.

Aside from the mindless tedium of the walking, Tigranes had the men to manage. They were accustomed to riding at a decent pace toward a definite destination along routes that passed through or near towns. They were not pleased to be plodding on foot through a dusty desert at a pace set by a family riding donkeys, with no idea how long they'd be at the task. Mostly they tried not to grumble, but as the miles wore on Tigranes found his patience wearing thin. There was a limit to how sharp he could get, though—out in this desert, separated not only from their company but from any civilization at all, his thread of authority was very long and very thin. His ability to govern the men was only as good as their internal discipline, and that was better in some than in others. This company had been chosen in torchlit haste, and if Tigranes had been given more time, he would have selected a different mix of soldiers. Most of them were decent fellows, but a couple were grumblers, especially a sullen, surly character named Diophantus. They had picked him up in Hatra to fill out their ranks after their losses at Alwenah, and Tigranes was increasingly of the opinion that they should have dropped him in Damascus. Diophantus was what Lord Gaspar wryly called a leadership opportunity, a challenge magnified by their separation and isolation, and Tigranes was wondering what he should do about the man. His grumbling and whining was annoying most of the others and infecting a couple of them.

The situation resolved itself in an abrupt manner on the third night of the journey. They'd found a broad hollow in which to camp, with the family sleeping not far off. What goodies the men had squirreled away from the feast had long since been consumed, and they were reduced to the soldier's staple: hard travel bread pulverized and cooked as a porridge, with scraps of mutton thrown in for flavoring. Diophantus started in grousing about missing bacon for the porridge, which was the usual flavoring. Tigranes took this as a subtle dig at his religion, and ignored it. Then Diophantus went on to grumble about the isolation of this duty, and how he couldn't wait to get to a proper town, and what he'd go looking for once he got there.

"Or maybe," he said with a snide smile. "I'll slip off and find that woman over there, and take her over the ridge for some fun. She's sure to be aching for more than that old man has to offer."

Tigranes didn't even think, so white-hot was his reaction. He only knew that he was suddenly kneeling on the soldier's chest, one hand at his throat and the other drawing a dagger.

"For that, your tongue goes first, *goishe* bastard," Tigranes growled. "Then I go for the other parts."

"Captain—no," came a calm but stern command. Looking up, Tigranes saw standing in the flickering light, just beyond the edge of the camp, Yusef holding his staff. What he was doing there, Tigranes did not know, but his quiet authority swiftly cooled Tigranes' searing fury.

"But...my lord..." Tigranes stammered. "He said –"

"I heard," Yusef replied. "It is of no matter. Please, let him go."

Tigranes could not deny that request, so he stood back. Diophantus scrambled to his feet and stood looking back and forth between Yusef and Tigranes, his eyes full of fear laced with humiliation.

"There," Tigranes gestured with his dagger. "You have the man you've so gravely insulted to thank for your life. But that's all you have. Leave your armor and weapons and go. Never let me see your face again."

Panic filled Diophantus' eyes, and he looked warily at Tigranes' dagger. He'd already shed his mail shirt, leaving only his pteryges and weapon belt. He fumbled at the buckle and dropped these to the ground, then scrambled backwards to the pile of gear, never taking his eyes from Tigranes. He frantically yanked his pack from the pile then ran off into the night, leaving the other soldiers stunned.

"I…I'm sorry you had to hear that, my lord," Tigranes said, sheathing his dagger.

"It is of no matter," Yusef replied. "A few rude words are not worth a man's blood."

"Would you like us to post a guard over your camp tonight, my lord? He may linger in the area, and attempt some mischief while you sleep."

Yusef looked into the night in the direction that Diophantus had fled. "No, Captain," he replied, shaking his head. "Thank you, but he will trouble us no longer. Let your men sleep."

Toward noon of the second day after that incident, they came over a rise and looked down on a village. The road ran down to it, where it joined a larger and busier road that curved away toward the southwest. Everyone smiled—this was clearly the road to Egypt. They had made it.

In the town Tigranes sent the men to find provisions, including a well-earned skin of wine. They ascertained from a shopkeeper that the Egyptian border was just a few miles hence, and a caravan of Jewish travelers was in the village, on their way to Alexandria. The caravan master was happy to have the family accompany them, so this was where the guard would turn back. For some reason, Tigranes found himself reluctant to make the parting.

"Thank you for all your protection, Captain," Yusef said with a gracious nod.

"It was an honor and a privilege, my lord, my lady," Tigranes replied, not caring who saw him bowing to a couple of peasants.

"Please extend our thanks to your masters as well," Miryam added. "Not just for their generosity, but for the honor of their visit."

"I shall, my lady," Tigranes answered. "In their name, if there is any further service I can render before we part –"

"Actually, there is one thing," Miryam replied, glancing over her shoulder toward the hill down which they had come. "Take back the man you cast out. He has been following us, hungry and thirsty."

Tigranes looked up the hill, where he caught a glimpse of a ragged shadow ducking behind a rock. He sighed and nodded.

"My stomach says to let him fend for himself. But at your request, my lady, I would do greater things than this."

"Thank you, Captain. Go in the *shalom* of the Lord."

Tigranes bowed again to the father and mother, and noticed that the baby in Miryam's arms was watching him with bright brown eyes. He gave a little bow to the child, then turned and walked away. He felt a curious mixture of crushed desolation and fresh hope, as if his whole life had existed for this task and now it was over—and yet, somehow, it was just beginning.

HOMEWARD

"Well done, Captain Tigranes," Gaspar commended the guard after receiving his report.

"Thank you, my lord."

"And well done to you as well, Baba," Gaspar added.

"Thank you, my lord," Baba said a little shyly. He still wasn't completely accustomed to being complimented by lords, but he was getting used to it.

Lord Gaspar smiled down at him gravely. "I'm especially pleased to hear that the final stage of the journey proceeded without incident. We've had more adventure on this journey than we would have liked, eh, Baba?"

"Yes, my lord," Baba replied, not looking at Captain Tigranes. He'd noticed that the captain's final report made no mention of Diophantus. They had taken him back, though not as a man-at-arms, and brought him here to Antioch, where he'd been quietly paid off and sent on his way.

"Hopefully our return journey will be even less adventurous," Lord Gaspar continued.

"Do we have any idea when that might commence, my lord?" Tigranes asked.

"That depends on how well Lord Melchior does," Gaspar sighed. "And our return trip will, I think, go forward in a different manner than our outbound one."

The sea journey from Joppa to Antioch had been short, but still expensive and cumbersome for such a large party with all their beasts. They'd been hosted in Antioch by an acquaintance of Balthazar's, but Melchior had fallen ill with a lingering cough. Balthazar spent much time sitting with his old master discussing many things, so practical governance of the caravan had devolved upon Gaspar.

Once this had become clear, the caravan's steward had come to Gaspar bearing scrolls and wearing a grave expression. The journey's expenditures had far exceeded the resources they'd brought with them, and they were in danger of being stranded hundreds of miles from home with no funds. Gaspar, whose military experience had included working with quartermasters and their dire predictions, sat down with the steward to go over the figures and come up with a plan. When they'd brought the plan to Melchior for his approval—most of the resources being his—the old mage had seemed remarkably unconcerned about the details, assuring the fretting steward that all would be well and turning the execution of the plan over to Gaspar.

Thus it was that many of the caravan's assets were sold off there in Antioch, including all the camels except Baba's favorite Xerxes. The men who'd been picked up along the way were paid off, and most of the men from Melchior's estate were sent home on horseback. Even with the winter rains, a company of light horse could make that distance within six weeks. The steward was one of them, and would return to Antioch with sufficient funds for the remainder of the company to return home.

This meant the three magi wintered in Antioch, with a reduced staff of attendants, which included Tigranes and Baba. At first there was much concern for Lord Melchior's health, as shortly after most of the company departed, he contracted a fever on top of his cough. For a few days it looked like he might not pull through. Balthazar and Gaspar were both concerned, not only by his illness but by the possibility that he might die so far from his lifelong home. But to everyone's surprise, this didn't seem to upset Melchior at all. In fact, the prospect of dying seemed to distress him far less now than the prospect of living had before they'd undertaken the journey. He spent a lot of time sleeping, or conversing quietly with his friends, or just gazing out his window and thinking—things the fiery, driven Melchior had never had any patience for before. He submitted to the ministrations of doctors without complaint, but seemed the least concerned of any of them about the outcome of their treatments.

Though he welcomed the other magi and would rally his strength to discuss important and profound matters, he seemed to most enjoy Baba's company, plying him with questions about the lives of the people of the estate—the families, their worries, their loves, their works. Melchior's only regret seemed to be that he might not be able to get back to the estate to see his people again.

For Melchior, a perennial topic of interest was the family of Beit-Lechem. He never tired of discussing every minute of the time spent with them, and pumped Baba for details of the journey along the edge of the Negev. Baba told him all he could remember of his conversations with Lady Miryam and Lord Yusef, almost wishing that more had happened so he would have more to discuss. It was a topic Lord Melchior never seemed to exhaust.

But Baba had other demands on his time. With the long winter days stretching before them, the magi took his education in hand. Lord Balthazar taught him how to read and write his native Aramaic, lessons in which he was joined by Captain Tigranes. Baba was also introduced to written Greek as well as basic mathematics. Lord Gaspar taught him geography and history, and he was amazed to learn that all the miles they'd traveled were but a small portion of the vast Roman world that stretched westward from where they were in Antioch. Then Lord Gaspar spoke of the lands further east from Baba's home, of his own homeland, the land of the Hind, and of far Cathay from whence came silk, and of island nations even further than that, until Baba's head reeled with the sheer vastness of the world.

Then the spring began to turn, and the chill, damp winter airs were supplanted by warmer breezes. Melchior began to sleep more soundly, and his breathing came easier. By the time the steward and his small escort returned from the estate, Melchior had regained much of his color and was walking more steadily. A couple of weeks after that, he was again able to mount his horse, and the doctors pronounced him well enough to travel at a slow pace.

So it was that on an early morning in May, a modest party of riders quietly slipped out of the gates of Antioch heading east. There was little remarkable about them—aside from a youth riding a camel, the party looked like nothing more than three gentlemen with a few retainers embarking on a journey. Nobody took note of them in the bustle of the traffic passing in and out of the busy city.

"Thus the last leg of our venture begins," Balthazar mused as they rode along. "So quietly, after our grandiose beginning, and all we've encountered."

Gaspar chuckled in response. "We old military dogs like quiet journeys—much preferable to the exciting ones. I'm content with slipping away unobtrusively."

Balthazar looked at Gaspar sideways. "I thought your dream was to have your name attached to something great and memorable. Surely this is the greatest thing any of us has ever done. Do you not wish even some of the glory?"

Gaspar thought a minute then shook his head. "It doesn't seem to matter anymore. It was enough to have even a small part in these doings. If my deeds are forgotten and my name lost, I will be content to have seen him."

Balthazar nodded in agreement. "As will I."

The slow passage down the length of Mesopotamia took two months. They were careful to stay well clear of Hatra, but other than that kept to the main road where accommodations could be found easily. Even with the pace kept slow for Melchior's sake, they made reasonable time, and rode up the last stretch of road to the gates of the estate just a couple of weeks past the summer solstice, before the heat of high summer set in.

There was great joy at the return of the master and his honored guests. Though the tale of the journey had already been told by those who had returned months earlier, it was told again at the great banquet which the head cook prepared in celebration. The estate buzzed with excitement and hope that things might be returning to how they'd been.

But it quickly became clear that this was not to be. Though Melchior had recovered most of his health, he did not return to the close management of the estate that had been his manner before the journey. He'd still receive the stable master, or steward, or whomever, but they'd quickly pass over whatever the report was and end up talking about the person's family, or interests, or hopes for the future.

"He's just as keen and interested as he ever was," the steward reported to Balthazar after one such meeting. "But he's keen about different things. It's like the estate—or the world itself—has lost its grip on him."

Thus it was that Balthazar took over much of the day-to-day management of the estate while Melchior strolled among the trees in the garden or helped the children feed the fish in the ponds. Gaspar stayed on at the estate as well, partly because he had nowhere else to go, but mostly because of a foreboding that something was imminent.

It was Tigranes who approached the two lords with his concerns about Melchior.

"It's not that he's sick, my lords. It's like he's—fading."

"Fading?" Gaspar asked.

"Well, thinning, perhaps. Like fog thins in the morning sunshine."

"Well, he has been seeking illumination all his life," Balthazar pointed out. "Perhaps he has found it, and taken it into himself."

Melchior lingered several months, losing none of his mental acuity but spending more time by himself. One evening his servant brought his evening meal to his room, only to find him missing. This sparked a panicked search of the grounds. It was Baba who found him collapsed on the steps of the observation tower.

"I wanted one more look," Melchior whispered quietly. It was approaching the autumn equinox, nearly two years after they'd first seen Jupiter approach Regulus. The magi and Captain Tigranes were summoned, and they assisted him to the top of the tower. There he sat on a chair, gazing at the starry hosts as a child would. The night was clear and the stars looked to be only a few feet above their heads. Melchior even reached up a few times as if to touch them, smiling mysteriously. Eventually he let himself be taken back to his room and put to bed.

Now it was obvious to everyone, especially himself, that the old magus was dying. He summoned his steward as well as several scholars from Seleucia to act as witnesses, and bequeathed his estate and all its contents to Balthazar. He would have divided it between him and Gaspar, but Gaspar declined. What followed was clearly a death watch. Melchior didn't wish to be left alone, or to see only doctors. He asked that all the estate residents come visit him in turn, down to the least stable boy. He spoke to them of their time on the estate and thanked them for their service, sometimes bestowing small gifts. It was while he was meeting with the woman who did his laundry that his breath caught, his eyes closed, and he slumped back onto his bed.

According to his wishes, Melchior was buried in the ground, after the customs of the Jews, rather than cremated or exposed like most Persians chose to be. A parade of nobles, dignitaries, and scholars made their way up the hill from Seleucia to honor his memory, speaking in glowing terms of all the great deeds that the great man had accomplished. Gaspar and Balthazar nodded and held their tongues, knowing that what the great man considered his greatest deed remained unknown to them all.

After the funeral Balthazar settled in as master of the estate. He and Gaspar discussed what to do—whether to restart the school that had once been Melchior's passion, or to run the estate as a simple country manor. In the end they decided to host what Balthazar called a "scholar's haven", where scholars from many schools could come and discuss their teachings and learn from one another. Invitations were extended to some of the scholars in the school of Bel'Tshazzar down in Seleucia, and word began spreading.

Gaspar stayed, first to help Balthazar get his footing and then to get the school started. But as the months turned into years, he began to feel a calling. The day came when he asked Balthazar to meet him by Melchior's grave, which was a slab of red-tinged marble at the west end of the garden.

"I've been thinking," Gaspar said. "That it's time for me to head for my homeland."

Balthazar nodded knowingly. "I've been wondering when this day would come. Sooner or later we all feel the call of our native soil."

"There's that, to be sure," Gaspar admitted. "But there's more. It's like I've got a task to do, preparations to make."

"Do you, now?" Balthazar asked. "Interesting, because I feel the same way. In fact, that's a good part of why I set up the scholar's haven—not as an end in itself, but in preparation for something to follow, something greater."

"Do you have any idea what?"

"No," Balthazar shook his head. "But great things are afoot in the heavens and on earth. We had the privilege of seeing the beginning of them; it's probably too much to expect that we should see their fruition."

"Indeed," Gaspar acknowledged, resting his hand on the marble slab. "I've been loath to break up our partnership, but in a sense that's already begun."

"In one sense, yes," Balthazar admitted. "But in another sense, never. We may be separated by years, miles, or even death itself, but in a way we will be ever kneeling together in that humble hut in Beit-Lechem. It is our burden and our glory."

Gaspar nodded and fell silent. They rarely spoke of that any more, even among themselves, treasuring the event in the silence of their hearts. At length he spoke again.

"I hope you don't mind if I offer Baba the opportunity to accompany me. He may not want to, but I want to at least given him the chance."

"With my blessing," Balthazar waved. "He has been your squire since we returned. It would be a crime to deny him the chance to stay with you. His family will find it hard, but I think they've seen this coming."

So it was that three weeks later, a small party rode out of the gate of the estate after tearful farewells all around. Gaspar had come to be loved and respected by all, and Baba was one of their own. The lad had grown into a tall young man who was known not only for his speed in the saddle and his skill with weapons, but for his scholarship and wisdom. These attributes, so uncommon in a youth, had drawn the attention of many maidens of the estate, who were now heartbroken to see him departing. But he deemed his place was with his master.

The small company rode down to the port at the mouth of the Euphrates. There Gaspar and Baba took ship for the port of Muziris, near Gaspar's home.

The years passed quickly. A local *kshatrapa*, recognizing Gaspar's knowledge and ability, appointed him head of his kingdom's forces. This enabled the *kshatrapa* to repulse his enemies on all sides and bring peace within his borders. But when his able general refused to embark on a campaign of conquest, the *kshatrapa* prudently decided that he'd rather retain Gaspar than enlarge his kingdom, and made him royal advisor on legal matters and diplomacy. In time, Gaspar's reputation spread, and judges and scholars came from kingdoms all around to learn from him.

Through all this Baba stayed by Gaspar's side—first as an aide, then as a lieutenant, and eventually as a general in his own right. In time he took a wife and started a family, and the now older magus was always welcome at their door.

It was at that door that the two men sat, decades later, relaxing in the evening breeze. They had grown old together. Gaspar had almost reached his eightieth year, and still retained his health and clarity of mind, though his eyesight was dimming. Baba was also healthy, having passed his sixtieth year, and his children were now bringing their children to him.

Their vantage point at the front of the house allowed them to look down the hill to where the river flowed through the port of Muciri. One of Baba's sons, Gobryas, who was a trader in the port, came ambling up the hill as the sun set.

"What news, son?" Baba asked, sliding aside to make room on the bench.

"Another Roman ship, bringing gold to buy pepper," Gobryas reported. "Also, a passenger."

"A passenger?" Baba asked. This was unusual—Romans came to the land of the Hind to trade, but not to stay.

"Just so. Not a Roman, but of some other race. He speaks Aramaic and a little Greek, though most of the merchants could not understand his vocabulary. Your skills may be needed." As a rule, most merchants learned only enough of other languages to conduct trade.

"Indeed?" Gaspar asked. "Did this Aramaic speaker give his name, or his business?"

"From what we could understand, he came to speak of some new god, one who died but lives again. He said he was from Jerusalem. His name is Thomas, or Didymus in Greek."

"Jerusalem?" Gaspar sat up and looked sharply at Baba.

"That's what he said."

"Really?" Gaspar mused. "Really, now? Baba, perhaps we should seek out this Thomas and learn more of his business."

ABOUT THE AUTHOR

Roger Thomas is a self-employed computer consultant and corporate instructor who lives in Michigan with his wife Ellen. They have raised six children and are now helping those children raise their 14 (at last count) grandchildren. He loves reading, especially works by the Inklings, and baking bread to enjoy with homemade grape jam. *From Afar* is his third book.

OTHER BOOKS BY ROGER THOMAS

The Accidental Marriage

The Last Ugly Person and Other Short Stories

Made in the USA
Middletown, DE
05 December 2016